DEATH BY
SMOOTHIE

Books by Laura Levine

THIS PEN FOR HIRE
LAST WRITES
KILLER BLONDE
SHOES TO DIE FOR
THE PMS MURDER
DEATH BY PANTYHOSE
CANDY CANE MURDER
KILLING BRIDEZILLA
KILLER CRUISE
DEATH OF A TROPHY WIFE
GINGERBREAD COOKIE MURDER
PAMPERED TO DEATH
DEATH OF A NEIGHBORHOOD WITCH
KILLING CUPID
DEATH BY TIARA
MURDER HAS NINE LIVES
DEATH OF A BACHELORETTE
DEATH OF A NEIGHBORHOOD SCROOGE
DEATH OF A GIGOLO
CHRISTMAS SWEETS
MURDER GETS A MAKEOVER
DEATH BY SMOOTHIE

Published by Kensington Publishing Corp.

DEATH BY SMOOTHIE

LAURA LEVINE

Kensington Publishing Corp.
www.kensingtonbooks.com

KENSINGTON BOOKS are published by

Kensington Publishing Corp.
119 West 40th Street
New York, NY 10018

Copyright © 2022 by Laura Levine

All Kensington Titles, Imprints, and Distributed Lines are available at special quantity discounts for bulk purchases for sales promotions, premiums, fund-raising, and educational or institutional use. Special book excerpts or customized printings can also be created to fit specific needs. For details, write or phone the office of the Kensington special sales manager: Kensington Publishing Corp., 119 West 40th Street, New York, NY 10018, attn: Special Sales Department, Phone: 1-800-221-2647.

The K and Teapot logo is a trademark of Kensington Publishing Corp.

Library of Congress Card Catalogue Number: 2022940966

ISBN: 978-1-4967-2816-6

First Kensington Hardcover Edition: December 2022

ISBN: 978-1-4967-2818-0 (ebook)

10 9 8 7 6 5 4 3 2 1

Printed in the United States of America

In Loving Memory of Benjamin Levine and Frank Mula

ACKNOWLEDGMENTS

As always, I am beyond grateful to my editor, John Scognamiglio, for his unwavering faith in Jaine. To my rock of an agent, Evan Marshall. To Hiro Kimura, whose cover art never fails to make me smile. To Lou Malcangi for another eye-catching dustjacket design. And to the rest of the gang at Kensington who keep Jaine and Prozac coming back for murder and minced mackerel guts each year.

A great big XOXO to my readers. You guys are the best (really!), and I'm grateful for every single one of you.

Finally, a special acknowledgement goes out to my best buddy, the late Frank Mula. Not only was Frank a sounding board for story ideas, he was a sounding board in real life, holding my hand and walking me through life's most difficult plot twists.

Whenever I got stuck on a joke, Frank (a two-time Emmy winner for his work on "The Simpsons") would come up with ten or fifteen others in the time it took me to run to the refrigerator for a work-avoidance snack.

His presence in my life—and my books—was a blessing, one I will always treasure and sorely miss.

Prologue

"Prozac Elizabeth Austen!" I cried as my cat dashed out my front door. "Get back here right now!"

The little devil had been pretending to be asleep on the sofa, but the minute I opened the door to get my mail, she bolted out like a shot. Lately, she'd developed a bad case of kitty cabin fever, eager to bust out of my apartment and wreak her special brand of havoc on my neighbors.

I was hot on her heels as she zoomed across the street.

Drat! She was heading up the Hurlbutts' driveway.

For some reason, Prozac seemed to be fascinated by Mr. and Mrs. Hurlbutt's house, scooting over there whenever possible to poop on their lawn and dig up Mrs. Hurlbutt's prize petunias.

Now I watched in dismay as she vaulted through their open kitchen window.

I caught up with her just in time to see her chowing down on a roast chicken Mrs. Hurlbutt had been foolish enough to leave out on her kitchen table.

"Prozac," I hissed. "Stop eating that chicken leg!"

Ever obedient, she stopped eating the leg and started in on the breast.

I was just about to climb in after her when Mrs. Hurlbutt, a plump sixty-something gal in a BEST GRANDMOTHER

EVER sweatshirt, came puffing into the kitchen, aghast at the sight of Prozac demolishing her chicken.

"Why, you little fracker!" she said, snatching Prozac away from the chicken and practically hurling her into my arms.

(To be perfectly accurate, the "f" word she used wasn't "fracker." But I'm keeping things clean for your delicate ears.)

As it turned out, the Best Grandmother Ever had one heck of a potty mouth.

After a string of expletives that would make a rapper blush, she proclaimed, "That little monster of yours has got to be the world's most infuriating cat!"

In my arms, Prozac belched proudly.

I try.

"I'm so sorry, Mrs. Hurlbutt. I'll get you another chicken at the market."

"If you don't keep that she-devil under control," Mrs. Hurlbutt threatened, her arms crossed firmly over her ample bosom, "I'm reporting her to the authorities."

I had no doubt she would. I could easily picture Prozac's face on the FBI's Most Wanted list. I left in a flurry of apologies and shuffled back home with Prozac in my arms.

"I can't believe you ate that chicken not fifteen minutes after scarfing down your Minced Mackerel Guts. How can one cat pack away so much food?"

Another satisfied belch.

It's a gift.

I was walking up the front path of my duplex on the low-rent outskirts of Beverly Hills when I ran into my neighbor, Lance Venable, dressed for work in a designer suit and tie, his blond curls moussed to perfection. As

Lance would be the first to tell you, he's one of the top-ranking women's shoe salesmen at Beverly Hills Neiman Marcus.

"I've got great news for you, Jaine!" he cried, following me into my apartment. "I'm in love!"

Oh, yawn. Lance falls in love about as often as most people change their sheets.

Now he was blathering on about his latest crush, an actor named Aidan, about how cute he was, how smart and funny.

"All that," he said, eyes shining, "and buns of steel!"

"Congratulations, Lance. But I fail to see how that's great news for me."

"I haven't gotten to that part yet."

"Get to it, please, sometime before I reach menopause."

As usual, my sarcasm went sailing over his blond curls.

"Aidan's just landed a part in a play, and they're looking for a writer to do punch-ups on the script. I told him about your many show biz credits, and he's recommending you for the job."

"Many show biz credits? What are you talking about? I wrote exactly one sitcom. And that was ages ago. I know nothing about writing plays."

"Neither do the producers. They're utter amateurs. So you'll fit right in.

"Anyway, you'll never guess what play they're doing. Remember the old sitcom *I Married a Zombie*?"

Of course I remembered. The actress who played the lead in that sitcom had lived up the street from us—a major league grouchpot, aggravating everybody with her nonstop complaints—until the night she got murdered. A murder in which, I'm sad to say, I was one of the cops' leading suspects. But that's a whole other story, one you can read all about, in *Death of a Neighborhood Witch*, available wherever fine books (and mine, too) are sold.

"That sitcom was a monumental flop," I said. "Who'd want to see a revival?"

"Apparently, it has a devoted cult following, and two of its biggest fans are producing it as a play. One of them won big money in the lottery. He and his girlfriend quit their IT day jobs and are using the lottery winnings to bankroll the production."

After giving me the producers' contact info and making me promise to send them my sitcom script, Lance air-kissed me goodbye and tootled off to fondle the tootsies of the rich and famous.

Somehow, I managed to ferret out my script in my computer files and sent it off to the producers, along with a cover letter and my résumé—the highlight of which was the Los Angeles Plumbers Association's Golden Plunger Award for my slogan *In a Rush to Flush? Call Toilet-masters!*

Admittedly, it wasn't much of a highlight, so my hopes were fairly low as I set out to buy Mrs. Hurlbutt her replacement chicken.

And yet, even though I knew it was a long shot, I couldn't help but feel a ping of excitement at the prospect of a play-writing gig.

Just think! Me, Jaine Austen, working in the thea-tah! What a welcome change from writing about Toiletmasters' double-flush commodes.

Suddenly, I had visions of living in some swank apartment in Manhattan, going to elegant opening-night parties, brunching with the stars, and soaking up the city's many cultural treasures—the museums, the symphony, the Everything Bagel!

By the time I checked out of the market with a roast chicken and Oreos for Mrs. Hurlbutt (okay, the Oreos were for me), I was fervently praying the producers would choose me for the job.

And, in what turned out to be a stroke of the worst possible luck, they did.

Chapter One

Of course, I had no idea of the disasters looming ahead when I drove over to meet the play's producers, Becca and David, a few days later. They'd read my sitcom script and liked it, and now they'd summoned me to meet them at the theater for an interview.

My destination turned out to be a slightly rundown venue on the outskirts of Hollywood whose marquee promised:

COMING SOON! I MARRIED A ZOMBIE!

The front doors were open, so I let myself in, walking past a dimly lit lobby to the auditorium. There I saw two people sitting in the audience as a pretty blonde looked over some script pages onstage.

I figured the duo in the audience were Becca and David, and that I'd caught them in the middle of an audition. So I slid onto a rumpsprung seat a few rows behind them.

"Ready to start?" David called up to the blonde.

"You bet!" she said, beaming a radiant smile.

With that, she started reading from the script as David fed her lines from his seat.

It was the scene where the play's leading character, Cryptessa Muldoon, freshly undead, bumps into a red-blooded young guy named Brad Abercrombie. He takes one look at her, and it's love at first sight. She tells him she can't possibly date him, that she's a zombie. But Brad, in a spate of Hallmark-inspired dialogue, insists he doesn't care, that love conquers all, and that somehow they'll make it work.

The young woman onstage was doing a terrific job delivering her syrupy lines.

When she was through reading, David asked her to sing a song from the play. She belted it out in a sweet clear voice:

> *Even though I was undead*
> *I couldn't bear to stay unwed*
> *I just about flipped*
> *When I stepped out of my crypt*
> *And saw him standing there.*
> *Never knew what I was missing*
> *Until we started kissing*
> *Things got hotter than hot*
> *Then we tied the knot*
> *Who would have thought a zombie*
> *Would wind up Mrs. Brad Abercrombie?*

Ouch. Somewhere Oscar Hammerstein was rolling over in his grave.

But in spite of the godawful lyrics, the actress still managed to pump some life into them.

"Great!" David called out to her when she was through.

"She's the best Cryptessa we've seen yet," I heard Becca whisper.

"We'll definitely be in touch," David said.

The blonde came down the stairs into the audience, thanking them profusely, and headed for the exit, beaming.

It was then that Becca turned and saw me.

"Hi. You must be Jaine. I'm Becca. And this is my partner, David."

They stood up to greet me, two uber-nerds in matching *I Married a Zombie* T-shirts.

Becca's tee clung to her generous hips, her lanky hair pooling on her shoulders, a fringe of bangs threatening to obscure her vision. In contrast to Becca's soft curves, David was painfully thin, a bundle of nervous energy, with taped-together glasses and a mop of wiry Brillo hair.

"David's not only producing the show," Becca said proudly, "he's also the director, writer, and leading man."

Talk about your renaissance geeks.

"Sorry to have kept you waiting," David said, getting down to business. "We're just wrapping up auditions. I think we should hire this last one," he said to Becca. "Katie Gustafson."

"Agreed," Becca said, making a note on a clipboard.

At which point, the door to the theater opened with a bang, and a spritely young thing came racing down the aisle.

"I hope I'm not too late to audition," she said.

David was staring at her, rapt.

And I could see why. She was one heck of a cutie-pie. Enormous Audrey Hepburn eyes, glossy brown hair pulled up into a high ponytail. With her elfin bod in leggings and a slouchy off-the-shoulder top, she was the very definition of adorable.

"No, you're not too late," David gulped, his eyeballs practically spronging from their sockets.

Becca eyed him warily. And I didn't blame her. If I had a boyfriend look at another woman the way David was looking at this cutie, I'd be wary, too.

"I'm Misty," the cutie said.

"Nice to meet you, Misty," Becca replied with a stiff smile. "Do you have a headshot and résumé for us?"

"Afraid not," the sprite shrugged. "I've never actually performed onstage before. But I've done plenty of acting as a waitress, pretending to like my customers."

"We were hoping for someone with a bit more experience," Becca started to say.

"But we're happy to have you read," David interrupted, handing Misty some script pages.

As she skittered up the steps to the stage, David's eyes were riveted on her perky little tush.

"Let's start from where Cryptessa meets Brad in the graveyard, the line where she says, 'Do you come here often?' "

"Okey doke," Misty said, and launched into her reading. "Smiling coyly, do you come here often?"

"No," David said. "*Smiling coyly* is a stage direction. You're not supposed to read it out loud. You're just supposed to smile coyly when you say your line."

"You mean like this?"

She shot David a very coy smile indeed. Coy bordering on pole dancer.

"Right," David gulped, his Adam's apple working overtime. "Like that."

Next to him, Becca's jaw clenched.

Misty proceeded to read her lines woodenly, mispronouncing words, utterly devoid of talent.

But David was staring at her, mesmerized.

Then it came time for her to sing.

It wouldn't seem possible, but her singing was even worse than her acting. I'd heard car alarms that sounded better than Misty.

When she was finished, a blessed silence descended on the auditorium.

"So how did I do?" Misty asked, looking directly at David.

"You stunk up the room faster than a rabid skunk."

Of course, no one said that. But I sure was thinking it.

"Uh . . . we'll get back to you," Becca managed to pipe up when she'd finally recovered her powers of speech.

"No need," says David. "You were fantastic!"

Huh?

"You're hired!"

"I am?" Misty beamed at David. "That's super!"

"How can we reach you?" he asked, a little too eagerly.

"Here's my phone number." Misty fished a lipstick from her purse and wrote her number in hot pink on the back of a crumpled Sephora receipt.

Then she flitted off, still beaming at David, totally ignoring me and Becca.

Once she was gone, Becca whirled on David.

"Are you crazy? She was awful!"

How true. Our little Misty had all the acting chops of a store mannequin.

"She's just unpolished," David said. "Nothing a good director can't fix."

A good director? Hah. Billy Wilder, Martin Scorsese, and Kathryn Bigelow rolled up in one couldn't turn Misty into an actress.

"David, you've never directed anything before. What makes you think you'll be able to wring a performance out of her?"

"I've never directed anything," David said, with a definite edge to his voice, "but I know I'll be good at it. Besides, we both agreed: I'm bankrolling this project, so I've got final say."

He seemed more than a tad ticked off.

"Of course, honey," Becca said, anxious to appease him. "I'm sure you'll be a great director."

Then they turned their attention, finally, to me.

But I could see both of them were distracted—David lost in what I was certain was a Misty-centric fog, Becca's eyes clouded over with worry.

"We really liked your sitcom script," Becca said, "and we'd love to work with you."

I have to confess I was having some doubts. From the little I'd heard, the dialogue was awful. And Misty in the lead was even worse. But then David said the magic words.

"How does $5,000 sound?"

Like music to my ears.

"I'm in!" I exclaimed.

"That's wonderful," Becca said. "I was afraid you'd be like the others."

"Others?'

"We've met with a few other writers," David confessed, "but none of them were available to take the job."

Okay, so what if I wasn't their first choice? And so what if every reputable writer in town had turned them down? A job was a job!

"Here's a copy of the script," Becca said. "It's running about fifteen minutes long, so we need you to make some cuts."

"Don't trim too much, though," David warned, clearly not thrilled at the prospect of losing any of his precious syllables.

I assured him I'd treat the script with kid gloves.

Then I practically skipped out of the theater, fueled by the thought of five thousand smackeroos headed for my checking account.

Chapter Two

I got in my car, still riding high over that five grand. Then, in the It Never Rains But Pours department, I checked my phone and saw a message from the Pasadena Historical Society, a prestigious bunch of old-money bluebloods. I'd applied for a job writing press releases for them months ago and had forgotten all about it. Now they'd texted me, wanting to set up a Zoom interview.

Would my good luck never end? Of course it would. But don't skip ahead any chapters to find out how. That's cheating.

Anyhow, I was a happy camper as I drove home that day, stopping off at the pet store to buy a present for Prozac. Fed up with my fractious fur ball dashing out the front door to wreak havoc on the neighbors, I'd decided to buy her a cat harness and take her for walks. This way she'd get to spend the time outdoors she so clearly craved, only I'd be there to make sure she didn't get into any mischief.

A rather brilliant plan, if I do say so myself.

"Hey, Pro!" I cried when I got home. "Look at this nifty cat harness! Now we can go on fun walks together!"

She glared at me from where she'd been snoring on the sofa.

Do you mind? I happen to be in the middle of a very important nap.

Okay, so she wasn't into it now, but she'd be very grateful once she was frolicking in the great outdoors.

As she rolled over and resumed her nap, I headed for my bedroom to freshen up. I had a dinner date that night with my BFF and loyal dining companion, Kandi Tobolowski.

Kandi and I met years ago at a UCLA screenwriting course, where we bonded over our mutual dislike of the instructor—a pompous blowhard who took far too much pleasure in trashing his students' scripts—and have been best friends ever since.

Soon I was tootling over to our favorite restaurant, Paco's Tacos, known throughout West L.A. for their home-made tortillas and burritos the size of the Goodyear Blimp.

My favorite dish on their menu was their chicken chimi-changas—crispy deep-fried tortillas, bursting with tender chicken, topped with a dollop of sour cream and guaca-mole—all nestled on a bed of black beans and refried rice.

Absolute heaven!

Kandi was already at the restaurant when I showed up, ensconced at a cozy table for two, checking her phone and nibbling on a chip. She's one of those size 6 gals who can make a chip last ten minutes. Not only that, she has silky chestnut hair that never frizzes in the rain.

But I love her anyway.

"Hi, honey!" she cried, catching sight of me. "I ordered you a margarita."

Sure enough, a bathtub-sized margarita, rimmed with salt, was waiting for me.

"Muchas gracias," I said, sitting across from her and taking a grateful sip. "So what's new?"

"The cockroach is in rehab again," she sighed.

The cockroach to whom she referred was a voice-over actor in the highly successful animated series *Beanie and the Cockroach*, where Kandi has been gainfully employed as a staff writer for the past several years.

"That guy has been in rehab so many times, they're going to name a wing after him."

A soft-spoken waiter appeared at our table just then, pad in hand, ready to take our orders.

"What'll it be, senoritas?"

"She'll have the tostada salad," Kandi said, "dressing on the side."

Was she out of her mind? No way was I having a salad for dinner.

"Only kidding," Kandi said, winking at me. "She's having the chicken chimichangas. I'm having the tostada salad with dressing on the side."

Of course she was. Which is why she was able to tuck her blouse in her jeans without emergency liposuction.

"So what's new with you?" she asked, still nibbling on the same chip she'd been nibbling on when I walked in the door.

(Meanwhile, I'd already polished off half the basket.)

I told her about my gig with *I Married a Zombie*.

"That's great," she said, raising her margarita glass in a toast. "Here's to your exciting new career in the theater!"

And with that, at long last, she finally finished her chip.

"I've got even more good news!" she said, eyes aglow. "We're about to meet the men of our dreams!"

"And just how is that going to happen?"

"My boss gave me two tickets to a bachelor auction. We get to bid on dates with L.A.'s most eligible bachelors!"

"Are you nuts? No way am I about to pay for a date."

"But they're the city's most eligible bachelors!"

"Kandi, this is Los Angeles. They don't call it Tinseltown for nothing. L.A.'s most eligible bachelors date models and actresses, not freelance writers in elastic-waist pants."

"You've got to stop being such a negative nelly. My boss went to the auction last year, and now she's engaged! It could happen to us!"

This was so typical of Kandi. An incurable romantic, she's always been willing to kiss a swampload of frogs in her search for Mr. Right.

I, on the other hand, after a disastrous marriage to a goofball extraordinaire whom I not so lovingly call "The Blob," am more than a tad jaded when it comes to romping in the minefields of romance.

"Sorry, Kandi," I said, slugging down some margarita. "Not gonna happen."

"But all the money goes to charity. You'll be doing a good deed."

"Tell me the name of the charity, and I'll write them a check."

Which I could afford to do now that I had that five grand waiting in the wings.

"Jaine Austen, you are such a party pooper. Why can't you ever think positive?"

"Because, as you well know, my dating karma stinks. I've had enough dates go up in flames to start a forest fire.'

"Everyone has bad dates. But that shouldn't stop you. You've got to look on the bright side and start visualizing what you want in life. It really works."

"Yeah, right," I replied with a cynical eye roll.

But Kandi wasn't about to give up.

"I want you to close your eyes this minute and visualize the man of your dreams."

I closed my eyes and gave it a shot.

"So?" she asked when I opened my eyes again. "What did you see?"

"Our waiter with my chimichangas."

Kandi groaned.

"Do you really want to go through life with your cat as your significant other?"

"Absolutely." I sat up straight, proud of my life as a singleton. "I don't need a man to complete me. Like Gloria Steinem said, 'A woman without a man is like a fish without a bicycle.'"

"Really? The same Gloria Steinem who's dated some of the world's most eligible bachelors?"

"Only because she's as pretty as a model or an actress. Sorry, Kandi. I'm hanging tough on this one."

"So am I," she said, doing a little spine stiffening of her own. "I'm not taking no for an answer."

With that, she grabbed the basket of chips and held it aloft, out of my reach.

"Not one more chip until you say yes."

Did she really think I was going to desert my principles for a few measly chips?

"So where is this auction, and what time should I be there?"

What can I say? Apparently, I've got guacamole where my spine should be.

You've Got Mail

To: Jausten
From: Shoptillyoudrop
Subject: Exciting News!

Exciting news, sweetheart! The annual Tampa Vistas talent show is just around the corner. It's always such a fun event. I can't wait to see Michele Serchuk clog dance. And Nick Roulakis play "Lady of Spain" on his harmonica. Our darling neighbor, Edna Lindstrom, is going to do the balcony scene from *Romeo and Juliet* with hand puppets! Doesn't that sound adorable? But the star of the show is sure to be our beloved president of the Tampa Vistas Homeowners Association, Lydia Pinkus, and her violin sonata. She wins first prize every year—and deservedly so.

Daddy claims Lydia bribes the judges. Which is absolute nonsense. But Daddy's always had it in for Lydia. Why on earth he dislikes her so much, I'll never know. She's such a lovely woman!

Anyhow, I made Daddy promise not to reprise the silly magic act he did last year. The only thing he made disappear was the audience.

Instead, he's decided to tap dance. The man has never tap danced in his life, but now he's taking an online course and is convinced he's Fred Astaire reincarnated. (Fred Flintstone, more likely.)

Meanwhile, his tappity-tap-tapping is driving me crazy.

Must run and get dinner started.

XOXO,
Mom

To: Jausten
From: DaddyO
Subject: Top Hat, White Tie, and Tails

Guess what, Lambchop?

Your very own DaddyO is going to be tap dancing in the annual Tampa Vistas talent show.

I've been learning online, and if I do say so myself, I'm a natural. With my talent and charisma, I'm certain to beat Lydia "The Battle Axe" Pinkus, who always manages to walk away with first prize for her boring violin sonata. (I suspect she's been bribing the judges.)

This year I'm determined to wrest the trophy from her stubby little fingers.

I'm renting a tux and dancing to Fred Astaire's famous "Top Hat, White Tie, and Tails." A simplified version, of course, but it's sure to impress. If only I had a way to spice up my act for that added "wow" factor.

I'm sure I'll think of something.

Gotta go. Mom wants me to run over to the market and get breadcrumbs for her meatloaf.

Love 'n snuggles from,

Daddy

PS. I still think I should've won the trophy with my magic act last year. It was sheer perfection. (Except for one tiny mishap when, instead of pulling a quarter out from behind Art Detman's ear, I pulled out his hearing aid.)

To: Jausten
From: DaddyO
Subject: The Perfect Addition

You'll never guess what I just found: the perfect addition to my tap dancing routine!

I was parking my car in the supermarket lot when I saw a man outside the market with a sign that read "Iguana for Sale." I was about to walk right past him, but then I realized the iguana was sitting on the man's head!

We got to chatting, and it turns out that Bob, the man with the iguana on his head, is moving to a new condo with a strict "No Iguanas" policy. It broke his heart to have to part with his beloved buddy, but he agreed to sell me Iggy, the iguana, for just fifty bucks. He assured me that iguanas make great pets and that Iggy would be sitting on my head in no time.

Just picture it, Lambchop. Me, onstage at the clubhouse, tap-dancing with an iguana on my head! Now that's entertainment!

I can practically feel the winner's trophy in my hands.

Love 'n hugs from
Your tap-happy,
Daddy

PS. Mom may be a tad peeved with me. In all the excitement of adopting Iggy, I forgot the breadcrumbs.

To: Jausten
From: Shoptillyoudrop
Subject: Unbelievable!

Unbelievable! I send Daddy out for breadcrumbs, and he comes home with an iguana!!

XOXO
Mom

PS. No meatloaf for dinner tonight. Daddy can fend for himself. I'm having fudge and chardonnay.

Chapter Three

When will I learn to never read my parents' emails on an empty stomach? I need to be well nourished, preferably with a calming glass of chardonnay by my side, to tackle the news from Tampa Vistas.

Daddy is a sweetie pie of the highest order, but a FEMA-grade disaster magnet, a walking, talking tornado of trouble. Poor Mom deserves a congressional medal of honor (or at least a lifetime supply of fudge) for putting up with his special brand of cray-cray. I cringed at the thought of him tap dancing with an iguana on his head, praying that the iguana would have the good sense to stay on the ground where he belonged.

I closed out my emails with a sigh, and after a restorative cinnamon raisin bagel slathered with butter and strawberry jam, settled down on my sofa to deal with yet another theatrical disaster.

Namely, David's script.

I knew his adaptation of *I Married a Zombie* was going to be bad. But I had no idea what a stink bomb royale it was until I started to read it.

Hacking through a jungle of feeble jokes, I was somehow able to decipher the story line—about a perky zombie

(Cryptessa) married to red-blooded human (Brad), both trying to keep her zombiehood a secret from Brad's stuffy dad—their efforts constantly thwarted by the antics of Cryptessa's mom, Catatonia, and her zany Uncle Dedly. In a preposterous ending, Brad's stuffy dad falls for Cryptessa's mom, and Uncle Dedly gets ordained as an online minister to perform a double wedding ceremony.

When I finished reading, I shook my head in disbelief.

David had managed the impossible. He'd written something even worse than the original TV show.

I was agonizing over what to cut, thinking the only possible answer was "everything," when I got a call from Becca.

"The actors are coming to the theater tomorrow at two o'clock to read the script for the first time. Why don't you join us? That should give you a better idea of what can be cut."

I was still voting for everything.

The next day I tootled over to the theater for the first table read, hoping David's wooden speeches would come to life in the hands of trained professionals.

Up onstage, two middle-aged actors were seated at a rehearsal table, looking over their scripts.

Nearby, Becca was talking to a slick hipster in tight jeans, black turtleneck, and tinted aviator glasses. As I headed down the aisle, I realized the hipster was none other than David. He'd had his wild nimbus of curls cropped into a stylish do and had traded in his dweeb duds for a whole new wardrobe.

What a change. From drip to hip, practically overnight.

Becca was dressed much as I'd seen her the other day, in baggy jeans and an I MARRIED A ZOMBIE tee.

They were deep in conversation as I approached.

"You're coming to dinner at my place tonight, right?" Becca asked, a pleading note in her voice.

"I'm not sure I can make it," the new David replied.

"But I'm cooking your favorite, spaghetti and meatballs. With chunks of cheese in the meatballs."

Sounded dee-lish to me, but David was far less enthused.

"Stop pressuring me, Becca," he snapped. "I've got a lot on my mind. If I can be there, I will. If not, I'll let you know."

Becca flinched at this verbal slap in the face.

I waited a few seconds before walking up the steps to the stage to join them.

"Hi, there," I said brightly, pretending I hadn't overheard their uncomfortable exchange.

"So glad you could make it, Jaine," Becca replied, forcing a smile. "Have you had a chance to read the script?"

"Of course she has, Becca," David said. "That's what we're paying her for. So what'd you think?" he asked, turning to me. "Great, huh?"

"Unbelievable," I replied. (Technically, not a lie.)

"Let me introduce you to our actors," Becca said, leading me over to the rehearsal table. "Guys, meet Jaine Austen. She's helping David with rewrites."

The two thespians looked up from their scripts with welcoming smiles.

"This is Delia Delacroix," Becca said, nodding at a regal dame with salt-and-pepper hair and cheekbones sharp as Ginsu knives. "She's acted on Broadway and the London stage."

"A pleasure to meet you, my dear," Delia said, her voice a throaty rasp.

"You probably already know who I am," said the actor sitting across from Delia.

Not a clue. But I smiled anyway, hoping he'd take that as a yes.

"This is Corky MacLaine," Becca said, coming to my rescue. "Corky played Cryptessa's husband, Brad, on the original TV show."

I vaguely remembered the leading man from *I Married a Zombie*, a clean-cut all-American guy with a headful of bright red hair.

The present-day Corky had gained a few pounds—and wrinkles—since those glory days. But his mop of hair was as red as ever, aided and abetted, I suspected, by a bottle of Clairol's finest.

When we were through exchanging hellos, Becca suggested that I help myself to some coffee and a pastry in the backstage kitchen.

I did not have to be asked twice.

Eager to check out the pastry (it had been a whole half hour since I'd scarfed down a quarter pounder for lunch), I headed backstage and found the kitchen, where a cute young guy was pouring himself a cup of coffee.

"You must be Jaine," said the cutie. "I'm Lance's friend, Aidan."

Tall and rangy, with sun-bleached hair and a taut, trim bod, he beamed me a blindingly white smile. I could see why Lance was so smitten with the guy.

"Thanks so much, Aidan, for recommending me for the job."

"Happy to do it. Although I don't know if you'll be thanking me when you read the script."

"Already read it."

"What a mess, huh? But who cares? A job's a job, right?"

"My motto exactly," I agreed.

"Want some coffee?" Aidan asked.

"No, thanks. I'll try a pastry, though."

I eyed a plate of disappointingly small brown muffins on the kitchen counter.

"I'd stay away from those if I were you," Aidan warned, as I started to reach for one. "They're gluten-free, fat-free, taste-free, and hard as a rock."

He picked one up and banged it on the counter. Nary a crumb fell off. In fact, I think it may have even scratched the Formica.

I eyed the brownish mini-boulders, and for once in my life, unwilling to break a tooth, I passed on a snack.

"Apparently, our Cryptessa is allergic to gluten," Aidan explained, "so David made me buy these. In addition to playing Uncle Dedly, I'm also the stagehand, prop guy, and all around gofer. If you need anything, just ask."

Another flash of that blinding smile.

"C'mon," he said, "let me give you a tour of the back-stage area."

He led me past a warren of tiny rooms, pointing out Misty's dressing room, the largest by far, especially compared to the broom closets allotted to Delia, Corky, and Aidan. Next to the tiny dressing rooms was an even tinier bathroom.

Passing a rusty metal door that looked like it hadn't been opened in decades, we arrived at a large area behind the set used to store props and equipment.

I looked around and gasped to see a mouse skittering out from a prop tombstone.

"Omigod, did you see that?"

"Yeah, we're having a problem with rodents. Becca's called the landlord to complain, but so far nothing's been done."

Eager to get away from that mouse, we scooted back out onstage, where Delia was checking her watch, impatient.

"It's past two-thirty. Where's our leading lady?"

As if on cue, Misty came rushing in just then, in jeggings and a lacy camisole top. I felt certain the camisole was meant to be worn as an undergarment, but Misty was wearing it solo, without a bra, leaving very little to the imagination.

"Sorry I'm late, guys," she said, sauntering down the aisle. "I slept through my alarm."

She slept through her alarm? At two in the afternoon? The girl must have one heck of a night life.

"And I had to stop off for my kale smoothie," she said, pulling a Styrofoam cup from her purse. "I have one every day. It's great for the complexion. You should try it, Becca. It'll clear up those zits in no time."

Becca blushed clear up to the smattering of zits on her forehead.

Then Misty turned her attention to David.

"Hey," she said, looking him up and down, "you sure clean up nice!"

David stuttered his thanks, gaping at Misty through his hot new aviators, lost in a lovestruck stupor.

"All right, everybody," Becca said, taking hold of the reins. "Let's get started."

We took our seats, joining Delia and Corky. David staked out a place at the head of the table, Misty hustling to sit next to him. Becca sat across from Misty as Aidan and I plunked ourselves down at the other end of the table.

David, finally roused from his stupor, cleared his throat to make a speech.

"Welcome, everyone, to the revival of *I Married a Zombie*, the first day of what I'm certain is going to be a smash hit, both here in Los Angeles and eventually on Broadway."

Dream on, buddy.

"Becca and I have been fans of *I Married a Zombie* for years."

Alert the media. He actually remembered Becca was still alive.

"We're thrilled to be able to mount this revival. And I don't like to toot my own horn, but I think my updated script is even better than the original."

Yeah, right. His script made the original piece of poo look positively Shakespearean.

"As you all know, I'll be directing and producing the show, as well as playing the leading man, Brad Abercrombie."

"Yay!" Misty clapped, David's own private cheerleader.

"I'll be in charge of all business affairs," Becca managed to break in before David started yakking again.

"I'd like to take a moment," he said, "to go around the table and introduce everyone. First, we're excited to have Broadway veteran Delia Delacroix playing the part of Cryptessa's mom, Catatonia."

"A pleasure to be here," Delia said with a gracious smile.

Misty stared at Delia, frowning.

"Isn't she too old to be my mom? My real mom is much younger than her."

Delia's gracious smile froze. Something told me she'd be putting in an angry call to her agent that night.

"And in a major coup," David continued, "we've got

Corky MacLaine from the original TV show playing Brad's father, Vern Abercrombie."

Corky smiled, waving hello to the others.

"Wait a minute," Misty piped up. "Didn't I just see you on an adult diaper commercial?"

Like Delia, Corky's smile froze.

Misty certainly wasn't about to win any popularity contest with this gang.

"Moving right along," Becca broke in, "we've got Aidan Rea, who'll be playing Uncle Dedly. Aidan has starred as both Hamlet and Willy Loman in his high school drama club."

Aidan nodded modestly.

"And across from Aidan is Jaine Austen, who's here to help David with script changes."

"Last but certainly not least," David said, "playing Cryptessa is our very special leading lady, Misty Baines."

He gazed at Misty adoringly, a gaze that went on way too long, until Becca finally said, "Let's do this, shall we?"

Picking up the script, she began reading:

"Exterior graveyard, Night. Cryptessa Muldoon, a beautiful young zombie, steps out from a mausoleum and bumps into handsome Brad Abercrombie, who's taking a midnight stroll through the graveyard . . ."

And so began what had to have been one of the worst table readings in the history of the theater. Delia, Corky, and Aidan were doing their best to resuscitate David's feeble script. Even David was trying not to sound like the rank amateur he was.

But all their efforts were undermined by Misty's monumental incompetence.

Not only was she still reading the stage directions aloud as part of her speeches, but she mispronounced the simplest of words. She couldn't even get her own name right, referring to herself as Cripetessa.

Delia sat gaping at her in disbelief. Never, I felt certain, had she seen such a lousy performance.

Trust me when I say the muffins were more entertaining than Misty.

The only time Misty even remotely came alive was when she was reading her love lines to David. Then she was all flirty and lovey-dovey.

Throughout it all, David was blind to her incompetence, laughing loudly as Misty mangled his bad jokes.

At last, mercifully, the reading came to an end.

"Great job, everybody," he said, staring at Misty, and Misty only. "You were terrific."

"Aw, thanks," Misty cooed. "But I'm still not sure of my lines. Maybe," she said, toying with one of the straps on her camisole, "you could come to my place and rehearse with me tonight?"

"Absolutely!" David replied, eager as a puppy for a Milk-Bone.

Becca watched the two of them, stricken.

Looked like she'd be eating spaghetti and meatballs alone that night.

Chapter Four

I think it's fair to say that Captain Ahab had an easier time duking it out with Moby Dick than I had trying to wrestle Prozac into her cat harness.

I'd read several articles on how to train your cat to walk on a leash, all of which said Prozac had to be hungry before training. So I waited until it was time for her midday snack before taking out her new harness and leash from where I'd stashed them in my hall closet.

She'd been yowling at my ankles, quite miffed that I wasn't in the kitchen opening a can of Minced Mackerel Guts.

The minute she saw that harness, she stopped yowling and began hissing.

Don't even think of trying to get me in that thing.

And that's when the battle started. You would have thought I was trying to strap her into the electric chair.

But I refused to give up, and after going at it for several rounds, sustaining an armful of scratches, I finally had her strapped in.

"Good girl!" I said, immediately tossing her a Kitty Kaviar treat. Which she gobbled up at the speed of light.

Then she looked up at me, indignant.

That's it? One lousy treat? For all my pain and suffering?

I took a step away from her, as instructed by my online gurus, and waved the bag of treats.

"Come here to Mommy, and get another yum-yum."

This was met with an outraged yowl.

That's extortion, pure and simple. I want a bowl of Minced Mackerel Guts, and I want it now! And PS. How many times do I have to tell you? You're not my mommy!

I pleaded with her to take just one tiny step, but she wouldn't budge an inch.

Instead, she hunkered down on the carpet, defiant, once again yowling at the top of her lungs. I was standing there, begging and pleading and waving the bag of treats when Lance came knocking at my door.

Wearily, I let him in.

"What's all the ruckus? I could hear Prozac out in the street."

"I'm trying to teach her to walk with a harness, but she refuses to budge an inch."

"You should have that looked at," he said, eyeing one of my more serious scratches.

"Honestly, Lance, that cat is absolutely infuriating."

Lance scoffed.

"Pro, infuriating? My precious sweet pea? Never! C'mere, hon," he said, beckoning to her. "Come to Uncle Lance."

And like Sleeping Beauty springing to life after a smackeroo from Prince Charming, the little traitor jumped up and went trotting over to Lance.

"Here you go, princess," he said, feeding her a treat and giving her a scratch behind the ears.

And get this. She actually rewarded him with a purr.

The duplicitous minx was sweetness and light with

everyone else on the planet. Only with me was she Lady Macbeth on steroids.

"So what do you say, Pro?" Lance asked, attaching the leash to the harness. "Want to go for a walk with Uncle Lance?"

She meowed happily, bounding out the door.

We made our way down the front path to our duplex, Prozac prancing by Lance's side, obedient as a geisha.

"How's everything going with 'I Married a Zombie'?" Lance asked as we headed up the street.

"The script is a wreck and the leading lady stinks, but it's a step up from writing about toilet bowls, so I'm happy."

"What do you think of my friend Aidan?"

"He seems great."

Lance's eyes lit up.

"Is he ever! And fabulous news! Aidan and I are about to become more than just friends. He asked me out to dinner! Well, technically, I asked him, but he said yes!"

"That's wonderful!"

"This is it, Jaine," he said, practically skipping down the street. "The big one. The Love Boat has finally docked at my pier."

I only half-listened to him ramble on about Aidan's fabulosity. How cute, smart, cute, funny, cute, witty, and cute he was.

Prozac, meanwhile, was trotting along, happily sniffing dandelions and dog poops.

At one point, she darted up a lawn to pounce on an unsuspecting bird, paying no attention when I called out, "Prozac, stop this very minute!" but coming to a screeching halt with a simple "No!" from Lance.

An elderly woman, seeing Prozac on the leash, stopped to admire her.

"If that isn't the cutest thing I've ever seen!" she exclaimed. "What a darling kitty."

Prozac preened.

Indeed I am.

"She's clearly devoted to you," the lady said to Lance.

I just sighed and let that one pass.

By the time we got back from our walk, Prozac had charmed several more pedestrians, and Lance was busy planning his first vacay with Aidan, trying to decide between Cabo or the wine country.

"Ciao for now," he said, handing me Pro's leash. "Gotta get dressed for my dinner date with Aidan! What should I wear, Jaine? Oxford blue stripe? Or black turtleneck."

"Oxford blue stripe."

"The turtleneck it is."

And off he sailed into his apartment. The minute he was gone, Prozac plopped down on the pavement, once again refusing to budge.

Beyond exasperated, I picked her up and carried her inside.

"What a little ingrate you are! On your best behavior with everybody except the one person who's kept you up to your eyeballs in Minced Mackerel Guts all these years. What on earth am I going to do with you?"

She looked up at me with lazy green eyes.

Feed me my Minced Mackerel Guts. That can isn't going to open itself, you know.

I swear, one of these days I'm going to trade her in for a gerbil.

Chapter Five

I spent the next several days working on David's script. Quel nightmare. Hacking away at his overblown dialogue was like trying to clear a forest with cuticle scissors.

I was slaving away on the rewrite when I got a frantic call from Becca.

"Jaine, you've got to come to rehearsal tomorrow. Ten a.m. We've got a real problem on our hands."

I'll say she did. Starting from Scene One, clear through to The End.

But it wasn't the script Becca was worried about, as I would soon discover.

When I showed up at the theater the next morning, the stage had been decorated as Brad Abercrombie's posh living room—except for a small corner up front where Aidan was setting up two papier-mâché tombstones for the graveyard scenes.

"Hey, Aidan," I said, heading up to the stage. "How's it going?"

He shook his head and sighed.

"Let's just say the most entertaining thing onstage are the tombstones."

"I'll bet," I commiserated. "Have you seen Becca anywhere?"

"I think she's in the kitchen with David."

I scurried backstage to the kitchen, and sure enough, I found Becca and David standing by a coffee urn, in the middle of a heated conversation.

New David looked quite spiffy in jeans and a motorcycle jacket, his curls gelled into submission. Becca, on the other hand, looked like she'd just spent the last several days flying coach behind a screaming toddler.

If the bags under her eyes were any indication, she hadn't been sleeping well—or at all.

". . . but she's awful," Becca was saying. "All the others have memorized their speeches, and Misty can barely pronounce her lines, let alone remember them. It's not too late to call Katie Gustafson."

I remembered the actress who'd given such a terrific performance at her audition.

"No way!" David snapped. "I know star quality when I see it, and I see it in Misty."

Let's all take a moment to roll our eyes at that one, shall we?

"She's sure to improve. After all, I've been coaching her one on one."

Talk about the blind leading the blind.

"I can't waste any more time discussing this," David said. "I've got more important matters on my mind."

Namely, how to worm his way into Misty's bed.

After lobbing me a curt nod, he hurried off, checking his reflection in his cell phone.

"Thank goodness you're here, Jaine," Becca said, catching sight of me. "Misty's messing up nonstop. You need to cut all her speeches so none of them is more than one sentence."

She reached into a cupboard for a bottle of Tylenol and popped two of them in her mouth.

"I've got the most terrible headache," she said, washing them down with some water from the kitchen tap.

I could only imagine.

"Help yourself to coffee," she said, "and I'll see you out front."

As I poured myself a cup of coffee, I noticed a pastry box on the counter. I opened it eagerly, only to find the same rock-hard muffins that had been served at the table read. In fact, they probably were the very same muffins. I doubted anyone had been brave enough to bite into one.

When I got back to the audience, I saw Delia and Corky had shown up—Delia sitting in the first row, doing the *New York Times* crossword puzzle, and Corky a few rows behind her, talking on his cell phone in a hushed whisper.

"Call me back as soon as you know," I heard him say.

Up onstage, David was discussing the living room set with Becca, telling her he wanted more throw pillows, an area rug, and a framed photo of Misty on the fireplace mantel.

"A framed photo of Misty on the mantel?" Becca asked. "No one in the audience will be able to see it."

"I'll be able to see it," David said. "It'll help bring my character to life."

What a load of bull. The only thing that'd help bring his character to life would be a real actor playing the part.

"Okay," Becca said through gritted teeth. "One framed photo of Misty coming right up."

I didn't have to be a rocket scientist to figure out that David and Becca's relationship, much like their play, was in deep doo-doo.

My thoughts were interrupted just then when Aidan walked up to me and handed me a menu.

"I'm taking lunch orders. What'll it be?"

Goodie. Food. That's usually a foolproof mood enhancer.

But not that day. The menu was from a joint called The Happy Veggie.

I groaned as I read a list of dishes that made prison food seem gourmet. Nary a burger or fry to be found. I knew I was in trouble when I saw the special of the day was tofu lasagna.

I chose the least noxious item I could find: an avocado and bean sprout wrap.

"Anything to go with that?" Aidan asked.

"A side of Tums."

"Tell me about it," he commiserated. "We have to order lunch from this place every day. It's Misty's favorite restaurant. Whatever Misty wants, Misty gets."

And it was quite clear, when she came strolling into the theater just then in jeggings and a midriff-baring top, that what Misty wanted—even more than tofu lasagna—was David.

"Hi, there!" she called out, ignoring the rest of us to focus a laser-beam smile on her producer/director/acting coach.

David's eyes lit up at the sight of her.

"Here she is!" he cried. "Our very own Cryptessa."

"Late as usual," Delia muttered.

And our very own Cryptessa kept everyone waiting another fifteen minutes while she went to her dressing room to get "centered."

At last, the rehearsal began.

I'll spare you the excruciating details (it's bad enough I had to sit through it) and just give you the highlights—I should say, lowlights—of Misty's performance.

For starters, she was *still* reading the stage directions

aloud. ("Sotto, we've got to keep our love a secret.") And, as Becca warned, she had trouble remembering the simplest of lines.

"You know what they say, Brad," she said making goo-goo eyes at David. "Love conquers . . . um . . . uh . . ."

"All!" Delia shouted, seething. "Love conquers *all*."

"Okay, okay," said Misty. "Chillax, grandma."

Throughout the rehearsal, she kept referring to Delia's character, Catatonia, as her grandmother. That, I was certain, she was doing on purpose.

And she actually had the nerve to take out her phone and text during the other actors' speeches. At one point, she even answered her phone when it rang.

"Sure, now's a good time to talk," she said to her caller. "What's up?"

"Do you mind?" Delia snorted as Misty continued chatting. "We're in the middle of a rehearsal!"

"That's okay," Misty replied. "I can still hear you fine."

By then, Delia looked like she was ready to personally dig Cryptessa a new grave.

Throughout it all, David was blind to Misty's lousy performance. After each scene, he gave notes to the others— *Delia, you need to be more imperious. Aidan, a scooch more zany. Corky, amp up that stuffiness*—but nada to Misty.

Every time she asked how she was doing, David assured her she was doing great.

Was he kidding? The little brat was single-handedly tanking the production.

At last, the glop passing as our lunch showed up from The Happy Veggie.

"You didn't forget to order my smoothie, did you?" Misty asked Aidan.

"Nope, Misty. It's right here."

He held up a large plastic container of viscous green goop.

"I'll put it in the fridge until snack time."

"Three o'clock sharp," she reminded him.

"Yes, *mein führer*."

Okay, he didn't call her *mein führer*. Not out loud, anyway.

Then she and David trotted off to her dressing room to "run lines."

Becca watched them head backstage, clearly miserable. The rest of us were thrilled to see them go.

Delia, Aidan, and I settled down on the sofa onstage to eat our lunch, while Becca remained out in the audience, working her cell phone to order throw pillows, an area rug, and that framed photo of Misty.

Corky, who'd practically torn out his red hair by the roots every time Misty screwed up, shuffled off to his dressing room to make some phone calls.

"Vodka, anyone?" Delia asked, whisking a flask from her purse and holding it out to me and Aidan. "I've resorted to the Smirnoff method of acting. It's the only way I'll get through this fiasco."

I was sorely tempted, but I passed on the vodka, as did Aidan.

"It's sheer hell having to take direction from David," Delia said, pouring a healthy dose of vodka into The Happy Veggie's herbal iced tea. "He actually thinks he's an actor! My God, if he were any more wooden, he'd have termites.

"And Misty!" she cried, on a roll. "What a skank. If she calls me grandma one more time I'm going to grab her by her jeggings and give her the wedgie of a lifetime."

"It's hard to believe anybody could be so dumb," Aidan said, "messing up her lines the way she does."

"Misty's not nearly as dumb as she's pretending to be," said Delia. "She knows exactly what she's doing. The more she screws up, the more time she gets to spend with David."

"But why?" I asked. "Why would a striver like Misty want an ex-nerdling like David?"

"Duh," Delia said, taking a healthy slug of her doctored iced tea. "The guy won the lottery."

"But he's putting most of the money into the play."

"Maybe Misty doesn't know that. Or maybe she's hoping she can scrounge a couple of grand out of him. Maybe she's not even in it for the money. Maybe she gets her jollies being the other woman and breaking up relationships."

Looking over at Becca on her cell phone, lost in a miasma of misery, I couldn't help but think that Delia might be right.

The three of us spent the rest of our lunch hour happily trashing Misty, or, as we were now calling her, Craptessa.

Somehow I managed to choke down my avocado and bean sprouts wrap, plucking out the sprouts whenever possible.

All too soon, David and Misty returned from Misty's dressing room, faint traces of lipstick on David's neck, Misty smiling smugly. At the sight of that smug smile, I was convinced Delia was right. Misty knew exactly what she was doing.

"Okay, everybody," David said. "Let's pick up where we left off." Then he looked around and asked, "Where's Corky?"

Just then Corky came rushing out onstage, a big smile on his face, looking animated for the first time all day.

"Great news! I just heard from my agent, and I've been offered a part in a big-budget movie. I'm sorry, David," he said, not looking the least bit sorry, "but I'm leaving the play."

"You can't quit," David protested.

"Watch me," Corky said, throwing on a windbreaker.

"I'll sue!"

"I don't think so," Corky countered. "A word of advice. The next time you want to be a producer, have your actors sign a contract."

"David, we can't stand in his way," Becca said. "It's a big-budget movie."

"And what are we—chopped liver?"

Actually, yes, but no one had the nerve to say so out loud.

"Bye, everybody," cried an elated Corky as he zipped up the aisle to the lobby.

"Good luck!" Becca called out after him.

He turned to look back at her, brimming with sympathy. "You, too, sweetheart. You, too."

"You'll be sorry when your movie tanks at the box office," David shouted, "and we're breaking box office records on Broadway."

"Aw, who cares?" Misty said. "You can do better than some guy who does adult diaper commercials."

"You're right," David agreed. "I *can* do better. You're fired, Corky!"

But Corky—lucky devil—was long gone.

"Okay, let's pick up where we left off," David said. "Becca, start lining up a replacement for Corky. And Jaine, you read Corky's part."

Rehearsals resumed, with me playing the part of stuffy Vern Abercrombie. I was terrible, of course, but not nearly as bad as Misty, who continued to stink up the joint, yawning and texting when she wasn't busy mangling her lines.

The rehearsal was lurching along, much like the *Titanic* after its run-in with the iceberg, when David, as the lovesick Brad, pleaded, "Cryptessa, won't you say those magic words I'm longing to hear?"

Cryptessa spoke, but not the magic words Brad was longing to hear.

"Ugh!" Misty cried in disgust. "A mouse."

And, indeed, a mouse was skittering across the stage. It stopped to sniff an errant bean sprout, but then, showing impeccable taste, turned up its nose and scampered away.

"I'm sick of these damn mice!" Misty whined. "Can't you do something about it, David?"

David whirled around to Becca. "Can't you do something about it, Becca?"

"I've called the landlord three times. He promised to send someone over soon."

"Well, make sure it happens," David barked, then picked up where he and Misty had left off.

"Cryptessa, won't you say those magic words I'm longing to hear?"

Once again, his wishes were about to be thwarted as Misty chirped:

"Time for my smoothie!"

Indeed it was three o'clock. And as they apparently did every day at three, things grinding to a halt while Aidan got Misty's smoothie from the fridge and brought it out to her.

Sad to say, the smoothie did nothing to improve her acting skills. She continued messing up her lines. That is, until it was time for Brad and Cryptessa to kiss.

David took Misty in his arms and for the first time all day, Misty got into the role, kissing David with a gusto usually reserved for soft-porn movies.

Out in the audience, Becca watched as the kiss went on way too long, her face a stony mask, except for the tears welling in her eyes.

Chapter Six

"Prozac, sweetheart! I'm so proud of you!"

Indeed I was. After much begging and pleading—and enough Kitty Kaviar treats to stuff a Bengal tiger—Prozac had actually allowed me to slip on her harness and take her for a walk. I even brought a scooper in case of emergency poops.

What a great idea this whole cat-walking thing had turned out to be. Not only would I be cutting down on litter-box duty, I'd also be toning my thighs!

"Wasn't that fun?" I asked Pro, when we were back in my apartment. "Walking together, bonding and pooping in the great outdoors?"

An impatient thump of her tail.

Yeah, right. Whatever. When do we eat?

I'd just tossed her some Kitty Kaviar goodies and was about to reward myself with a celebratory Oreo when the phone rang.

"You all set for today?" Kandi's voice came sailing over the line.

"Today?" I echoed, puzzled.

"The bachelor auction. You forgot all about it, didn't you?"

"Of course not," I lied.

It had totally slipped my mind. I only agreed to go to the dratted auction because Kandi had been holding my chips ransom at Paco's Tacos. The last thing I wanted was to watch a bunch of smug bachelors strut their stuff in front of an audience of desperate women.

"Meet me at noon," Kandi was saying. "Luncheon at the Beverly Wilshire."

Whoa, Nelly. Did someone say lunch? At the uber-posh Beverly Wilshire Hotel?

I remembered Kandi saying that her boss had paid for the tickets. Which meant free food.

Suddenly, I was raring to go.

I'd simply show up at the auction and chow down without bidding on anyone.

"Count me in!"

The minute I hung up, I raced to my bedroom and scoured my closet for something to wear. After much deliberation, I decided on a flowing white silk blouse, paired with black crepe pants, silver hoop earrings, and my one and only pair of Manolos—an outfit suitable (I hoped) for the rarified air of the Beverly Wilshire Hotel.

I set out in my Corolla feeling quite glam—until I looked down and noticed a bright red ketchup stain on the sleeve of my white silk blouse.

Damn it all. How did that get there?

Sometimes I think ketchup stains sprout on my clothes in the middle of the night, like mushrooms in the rain.

There was no time to turn back and change.

Oh, well. The stain wasn't that big, and if I kept my arm at my side, I was pretty sure no one would notice it.

Kandi was waiting for me in the lobby when I showed up at the hotel.

"Jaine, sweetie," she cried, giving me a hug. "You look terrific!"

See? I told you no one would notice.

"Except for that ketchup stain on your sleeve. But don't worry. No one will see it. All eyes will be riveted on the handsome hunks up for auction."

We made our way to the banquet room, awash in linen-clad tables, tasteful floral centerpieces, and thin women with fat checkbooks.

Kandi and I were seated at a table with four biz gals, all impeccably groomed, sans ketchup stains.

We'd each been given a program with glossy pictures and brief bios of the bachelors. As the other gals debated the merits of the men, I was busy studying the most important thing at the table: The menu.

We had a choice of poached salmon, kale caesar salad, or roast chicken with garlic mashed potatoes.

No contest there. Chicken with garlic mashed potatoes for *moi.*

And my heart did a flip-flop when I saw that one of the desserts was chocolate mousse cake. If there's one thing I love more than chocolate mousse cake, it's free chocolate mousse cake.

I silently blessed Kandi and her generous boss for inviting me to this fab event.

Kandi, of course, hadn't even glanced at the menu, too busy studying the bachelors.

"It's a toss-up," she said, "between Ethan, a stockbroker who loves to cruise the Caribbean in his yacht, and Ross, one of the top three real estate brokers in Los Angeles.

"Do I want a life at sea," she mused, "cruising the Caribbean? Or someone to get me top dollar for my condo if I ever decide to sell it?"

After a lively debate with herself about the merits of Ethan versus Ross, she finally decided to go with Ethan, the yachtsman.

"I've never been sailing before," Kandi said, dreamy-eyed, already mentally cruising the high seas. "It's something I've always wanted to do. And what about you?" she asked me, snapping out of her daydream. "Have you made up your mind?"

"You bet. I'm having the roast chicken with garlic mashed potatoes and chocolate mousse cake for dessert."

"Jaine," she sighed, exasperated, "have you even looked at the program?"

"Yeah, just now, when you showed me Ethan's picture."

"Aren't you going to bid on anyone?"

"I wasn't planning to."

I sensed some serious arm-twisting coming on, but was rescued just then when the waiter showed up to take our orders. All the other gals at the table, having taken leave of their senses, ordered the kale caesar salad. (Can you believe there are women on this planet who actually choose to eat salad for lunch? With dressing on the side?)

Needless to say, I was the only who ordered roast chicken and garlic mashed potatoes.

I mean, somebody's got to support the mashed potato industry, right?

Once our orders were taken, the auction began, with one eligible bachelor after another strutting his stuff up onstage. All dressed in designer suits, groomed to perfection, radiating confidence and testosterone.

The bidding was lively, to say the least, hands shooting up like pistons in a race car.

Nobody but me was even paying attention to the food when it showed up.

Yes, it appeared that I was the only person in the room who was actually eating. And I'm happy to report that the roast chicken and garlic mashed potatoes were divine.

Bonus good news: Because everyone at our table was ignoring our basket of warm, crunchy sourdough rolls, I got to carbo load big time.

Kandi had barely made a dent in her salad when Ethan, her yachtsman, came out onstage. He really was a looker—tall and blond and Nordic, straight out of a Ralph Lauren photo shoot.

Apparently Kandi wasn't the only one in the room with the hots for him. The bidding was heavy, women shouting out frantic offers. As the price tag got higher and higher, one by one the women began dropping out. Until the field had narrowed down to Kandi and one other gal at our table, a sleek brunette with a nose so minuscule, it had to have come from a plastic surgeon.

By now, the cost of a date with Ethan had soared up to $4,000.

"$4,500. Do I hear $4,500?" called the auctioneer.

Kandi's hand shot up.

"$5,000," cried Ms. Nose Job.

"$5,500," countered Kandi.

"Are you nuts?" I said, tugging her arm. "You can't spend $5,500 on a date!"

"It's okay," she said, a feverish gleam in her eyes. "I can cash out a CD."

"$6,000?" the auctioneer asked.

I had to end this madness once and for all and stop the price from escalating any further.

"Omigosh!" I cried to Ms. Nose Job, just as she was about to raise her hand to outbid Kandi. "Is that a spider on your leg?"

"A spider?" she gasped, horrified.

She looked down at her legs, and as she checked for crawling insects, the auctioneer called out "Sold!" to Kandi.

"I won!" she cried. "I won!"

Ms. Nose Job looked up from her leg and glared at me.

"My mistake," I said. "It wasn't a spider, after all. It's just a mole."

For a minute, I feared Ms. Nose Job was going to dump her kale caesar salad on my head.

Meanwhile, Kandi was in seventh heaven.

And so was I, because just then the waiter showed up with our desserts. Everyone else at the table had ordered either sherbet or biscotti. What fools! Only I had been discerning enough to order the chocolate mousse cake.

So you can imagine my dismay when the waiter slapped down a plate of biscotti in front of me. I turned to tell him of his mistake, but he was already scooting away to another table.

"Wait!" I cried. "Where's my chocolate mousse cake?"

I was waving my hand to get his attention when I heard the auctioneer call out:

"Sold for $600 to the woman with a ketchup stain on her sleeve!"

Dammit. When I waved my hand, the auctioneer thought I was making a bid.

Of course, he didn't really mention the ketchup stain, but all the ladies at my table were staring at it.

It looked like I'd just bid $600 on a guy named Skyler, who, according to the program notes, was an entrepreneur and patron of the arts.

True, he was suave and dark and classically handsome, with slicked-back hair and a fancy designer suit, but too much of a biz guy for me. Probably liked to sit around yakking about the Dow Jones Industrial Average. A far cry from the artsy creative types I usually fall for.

Kandi, seeing my distress, insisted on picking up the tab.

But I couldn't let her.

As much as I hated to part with the dough, technically I

could afford it, thanks to my *I Married a Zombie* pay-check. And besides, the money was going to charity.

I was more than a tad chagrined, however, when I learned that the charity in question was a scholarship fund for the Gwyneth Paltrow School of Organic Cosmetology. So, in the end, I wound up paying money I hated to lose to a charity I couldn't care less about for a date I didn't want in the first place.

But on the plus side, my chocolate mousse cake, when it finally showed up, was delicious.

(And so were the biscotti.)

You've Got Mail

To: Jausten
From: Shoptillyoudrop
Subject: Free Range Iguana

I could positively strangle Daddy for bringing home that dratted iguana! Not only has he been using my best butter lettuce for Iggy's "snacks," he's let the scaly creature roam around the house at will. Daddy says it's not fair to keep him cooped up in his cage, insisting that Iggy is a "free range" iguana.

I can't tell you how many times I've been walking along, minding my own business, only to have Iggy come darting out in front of me like a mini-Godzilla, scaring me half to death.

Today I laid down the law and ordered Daddy to return Iggy to the charlatan who sold it to him. But Daddy begged me to let him keep Iggy until after the talent show, and in a moment of weakness, I said yes.

So, for the time being, I'm stuck with Godzilla Lite.

Who, incidentally, will definitely not be roaming "free range" this Thursday when my book club ladies come to the house for lunch. Iggy will be locked in his cage in the guest bedroom. The last thing I need is an iguana joining our discussion of *Wuthering Heights*. Which, I'm ashamed to admit, I haven't even come close to finishing. (I must remember to rent the movie version from the library.)

Ugh. Daddy just started his godawful tappity-tap-tapping. It's like a herd of elephants running through the house. No wonder I can't concentrate on *Wuthering Heights.*

XOXO
Mom

PS. Fingers crossed Daddy can't train Iggy to sit on his head and gives up his crazy tap-dancing-with-an-iguana scheme. The sooner that bubble bursts, the happier I'll be.

To: Jausten
From: DaddyO
Subject: Fabulous News!

Fabulous news! I just got Iggy to sit on my head. He actually seems to like it up there and stayed perched in place throughout my dance. I tell you, Lambchop, Iggy is a natural, a born entertainer—just like me!

And this talent show is just the beginning. I smell stardom heading our way.

Love 'n snuggles from,
Daddy

To: Jausten
From: Shoptillyoudrop
Subject: Darn It All!

Darn it all. It turns out Iggy likes sitting on Daddy's head. So Daddy is more determined than ever to tap dance his way to humiliation at the talent show.

In the meanwhile, if he thinks I'm going anywhere near him after he's had an iguana lounging on his head, he's got another think coming. No kissing, no cuddling—and definitely no running my fingers through his hair!

XOXO
Mom

To: Jausten
From: DaddyO
Subject: Finishing Touch

You'll never guess what I just ordered online. A miniature top hat for Iggy! The perfect finishing touch to our blockbuster dance act!

I can't wait to tell Mom!

Love 'n kisses,
Daddy

To: Jausten
From: Shoptillyoudrop
Subject: Round the Bend

It's official. Daddy has gone round the bend. The man just ordered a top hat for an iguana.

In desperate need of fudge—
Mom

Chapter Seven

I was still reeling from the sticker shock of my $600 lunch—not to mention the thought of Daddy tap dancing with a top-hatted iguana—when Becca called later that afternoon.

"Tensions on the set have been running a bit high," she said.

A bit high? Last I saw, it was practically a war zone.

"So David and I have decided to host a morale-boosting dinner tomorrow night. I hope you can join us."

"Um . . . sure," I said, not exactly thrilled at the prospect of hanging with the *Zombie* crew.

"Great! See you tomorrow, seven-thirty at Trattoria Italiana in West Hollywood. And, by the way, Misty's still having trouble with her lines. So can you cut her speeches down to words of three syllables or less?"

Yikes. At the rate Misty was going, she'd soon be doing her performance in pantomime.

I was hard at work the next day, hacking syllables from Misty's speeches, when Lance came knocking at my door.

He bounded in, his blond curls practically quivering with excitement, blathering about his date with Aidan, how it was "magic, sheer magic." He went on to describe in excruciating detail their dinner at the beach, splitting a bottle of chardonnay (or cabernet), how the scallops (or scallions) were divine, and how they ended the date with a kiss (or a knish).

I wasn't really listening.

"Anyhoo," Lance said, finally coming back down to earth, "Aidan tells me you'll be seeing him tonight at an *I Married a Zombie* dinner."

"That's right."

"Well, just in case it comes up, I might have exaggerated a few things about my life when I chatted with Aidan."

"Such as?"

"Such as I told him I was head of Neiman's shoe department and best buddies with Jimmy Choo."

"You're best buddies with Jimmy Choo, the world-renowned shoe designer who lives in London?"

"And Salvatore Ferragamo."

"Lance, I'm pretty sure Salvatore Ferragamo is dead."

"Must you be such a nitpicker?" Lance huffed. "Just back me up on my fibs, will you?"

Calling Lance's monumental whoppers "fibs" was like calling King Kong a chimpanzee, but I agreed not to spill the beans.

As it turned out, I didn't have to worry about backing up Lance's whoppers at dinner that night because Aidan was way too busy trashing Misty to chat about Lance.

When I showed up at the trattoria—a cozy joint with Chianti bottles on the tables, Italian landscapes on the wall, and Dean Martin crooning over the sound system—I found Aidan and Delia at a table with banquette seating on one side and chairs on the other.

They were the first to arrive, sitting across from each other, Aidan on the banquette with a beer, Delia in a chair, swathed in black chiffon and plucking an olive from a very large martini.

"Hi, guys," I said, sitting in the chair next to Delia.

"Hey, Jaine," Aidan treated me to a bolt of his mega-watt smile. "Welcome to our morale-boosting dinner."

"The only way to boost morale on this production," Delia said, popping the olive in her mouth, "would be to catapult Misty out of a cannon."

"I'd pay big bucks to see that," Aidan chimed in.

"The little brat still hasn't bothered to learn her lines," Delia groaned. "Honestly, I've worked with dogs who learned their parts faster."

"And would you believe," Aidan added, "I've got to pick up her dry cleaning?"

"Now she's giving acting notes on what's working and what's not working," said Delia, taking a healthy slug of her martini. "What's worse, David's actually listening to her."

"But we get our revenge," Aidan said. "We take turns spitting in her smoothie!"

"It's the high point of my day," Delia grinned. "Oh, look. Here comes Craptessa now."

I turned to see Misty coming our way in jeggings and a slouchy top, her ponytail and big doe eyes lending her a deceptive air of innocence.

She slid onto the banquette, yakking on her phone, not even bothering to acknowledge our presence.

"Yeah, everything's going great. He's so into me. Becca's totally toast. I'll tell you everything when I see you. But I can't talk now. I'm not alone." She finally bothered to glance our way. "Nobody important. Just some people from the play. Oops. Gotta run. David's coming."

And, indeed, David and Becca had just shown up with a handsome fiftysomething silver fox in tow.

David was going for the Steve McQueen look in a bomber

jacket, tight jeans, and tinted aviators, while Becca remained true to her baggy jeans and *I Married a Zombie* tee.

"Hi, everybody!" Becca said. "I'd like you to meet Corky's replacement, Preston Chambers."

"A pleasure to meet you all," said our newest cast member. With his thick mane of silver hair and urbane good looks, he was the kind of Aarpster hottie you see in brochures for cruise ships and brokerage houses. "So happy to be part of the show."

"You won't be for long," Delia muttered under her breath.

"Why don't you sit on the banquette next to Misty," Becca said to Preston. "David and I will sit here," she added, gesturing to the two open chairs.

"No," Misty protested. "I want David to sit here," she said, patting the banquette. "Next to me."

David didn't have to be asked twice. Like a lap dog being summoned by his mistress, he scrambled to the banquette and scooched over to Misty.

Becca gritted her teeth as she sat down next to me in one of the chairs, the silver fox sitting next to her.

By now, David had scooted so close to Misty, he was practically sitting in her lap. Finally managing to tear his eyes away from her, he introduced us all to Preston, taking extra time to sing Misty's praises.

"She's doing a fantastic job as Cryptessa."

"Oh, brother," I could hear Delia say as she polished off her martini.

"Preston has just come from a successful run of *A Doll's House*," Becca said.

The silver fox smiled modestly.

"The Dolls' House?" Misty said. "You mean that strip club in Burbank?"

"No, darling," Delia said to Misty. "*A Doll's House* is a play by Henrik Ibsen. If I can find a comic book version, I'll get you a copy."

"Plays are such a snore," Misty said, ignoring Delia's zinger. "Except for yours, of course, David. Yours is really fun."

"It does break the mold, doesn't it?" David said.

"Causes mold, more likely," Delia muttered.

Our waiter showed up at the table just then to take the rest of our drink orders.

Delia wasted no time ordering another martini.

"And I'll have a bottle of chardonnay," I said.

Okay, I didn't really order a whole bottle. But trust me. I was tempted.

"I'll have a double scotch on the rocks," Becca said.

"Make that two," Preston chimed in, a man clearly in need of alcoholic fortification.

David looked over at Becca, surprised.

"But, Becca. You don't drink."

"I do tonight," she said, a steely glint in her eyes.

"I'll have a Herradura margarita," Misty said. "No salt. If I see even a speck of salt on the rim," she threatened, "I'm sending it back."

Why did I get the feeling that our waiter would soon be carrying on Delia and Aidan's proud tradition of spitting in Misty's drink?

With a stiff smile, he passed out menus.

Misty looked at hers, scrunching her nose in dismay.

"We're at an Italian restaurant?"

"Yes, Misty," Delia said as if talking to a four-year-old. "I think any restaurant called Trattoria Italiana can safely be assumed to be Italian."

"Where are the vegan dishes? I'm vegan, you know."

"We know," Delia, Aidan, and Becca sighed in unison.

"I want to eat at a vegan restaurant. I know a nice one not far from here."

"Do you?" David said. "Maybe we should go there."

"We are not going anywhere," Becca snapped, for once standing up to David. It appeared she'd grown a backbone under her *I Married a Zombie* tee. "We're staying here. Misty can order pasta."

"As long as it's gluten-free," Misty whined.

I got the feeling Becca was *thisclose* to bonking Misty over the head with a Chianti bottle, but just then a looker of a guy—who, unlike David, actually bore more than a passing resemblance to Steve McQueen—came storming up to our table.

Misty looked up, alarmed.

"What are *you* doing here?"

"You conniving bitch," Steve McQ sputtered. "I can't believe you dumped me for the jerk who's producing your play."

"David is not a jerk!" Misty cried, putting a protective arm around David's shoulder.

"And I'm not just the producer," David added in a burst of unwarranted egomania. "I'm also the director, writer, and leading man!'

"Just watch your back, dude," Misty's ex replied. "She'll rob you blind. I gave her two grand to pay her mom's medical bills. Only it turns out her mom is alive and well and dealing blackjack in Vegas. Our little Misty used the money to buy herself a Fendi handbag."

"That's a lie! It was Prada, not Fendi. And my mom really did have medical bills for her Botox injections."

"I hope your new boyfriend will have fun bringing you your damn smoothies every day, you lowlife, narcissistic piece of trash. I'm sorry I ever let you into my life.

"And PS," he shouted as he stormed out of the restaurant. "You stink as an actress!"

"I'll drink to that," Delia said, holding her martini glass aloft with a wicked grin.

I glanced over and saw Aidan and Becca, and even Preston, who'd known Misty less than fifteen minutes, grinning, too.

At last, someone had told off Misty in no uncertain terms.

Whaddaya know? Looked like this was a morale-boosting dinner after all.

Chapter Eight

"So?" Lance asked eagerly. "What did Aidan say about me last night?"

He was sitting next to me on my sofa the next morning, having barged in just as I was about to eat my breakfast, helping himself to half of my cinnamon raisin bagel.

"He didn't say anything, Lance. The dinner was about the play, not about you."

"Surely he must have said *something*," he pouted.

"Nothing. Nada. Zip."

He slumped down onto my sofa, crestfallen.

Prozac, who'd been snoozing on my armchair, belching on minced mackerel fumes, now stirred from her slumber and came trotting over to jump on Lance's lap.

"You're such a comfort to me, Pro," Lance said, scratching her behind her ears.

She gazed up at him with languid eyes.

Of course I am. Just keep scratching.

"I've been telling everybody I know about Aidan," Lance said, "even the checkout lady at the supermarket. She thinks we should go to Cabo on our honeymoon, by the way."

"You told the supermarket checker about Aidan?"

"Yes, Jaine. That's what you do when you're in love."

"No, Lance. That's what *you* do. Most people wait to see if they're actually in a relationship before they start planning their honeymoon."

My words of wisdom went unheeded.

"If Aidan didn't even mention me last night, clearly he doesn't care about me the way I care about him. I thought for sure we'd made a love connection, but I was wrong. It's just another failed romance to add to my dating résumé."

"Are you going to eat that?" I asked, pointing to his half of my cinnamon raisin bagel, which lay abandoned on the coffee table.

"Good grief, Jaine. How can you think about food at a time like this?"

Easy peasy. I do it all the time. But in deference to his grief, I refrained from snatching it up.

"Face it," he moaned. "I'm never going to find anyone. Or go on that honeymoon in Cabo. My life is over. Finished. Kaput. I might as well join a monastery."

He was roused from his pity party just then when his cell phone dinged with a text.

"It's from Aidan!" he said, suddenly springing back to life. "He wants to meet for dinner tonight. Cancel that monastery. Time to hit the gym!"

Prying Prozac from his lap, he leaped up from the sofa and scooted out the door, happily munching on my cinnamon raisin bagel.

I swear, a person could get whiplash keeping up with his mood swings.

I myself was in a particularly jolly mood that morning.

Today was the day of my Zoom interview with the Pasadena Historical Society.

Pasadena is one of L.A.'s oldest neighborhoods, rife

with fabulous Victorian and American Craftsman houses. And the mission of the Pasadena Historical Society, according to their website, is to protect and preserve those architectural treasures, conducting house tours and lectures and fundraising galas.

A job from these old-money bluebloods would give my writing credits a much-needed touch of class.

In an effort to look refined, I chose to wear a blue cashmere sweater accessorized with a tasteful string of pearls. After my fashion faux pas at the bachelor auction, I carefully checked the sweater for ketchup stains. Only when I was certain it was ketchup-free did I put it on.

I didn't bother changing out of my pajama bottoms—festooned with kittens in teacups—knowing I'd be seen only from the waist up on my Zoom chat.

With just a hint of makeup and my mop of curls tamed into submission, I hoped I looked like the kind of gal who had her name on the social register and not on the Fudge of the Month Club mailing list.

At the designated time, I took a seat at my computer in the dining room, checked my sweater one last time for ketchup stains, then clicked on the invitation to chat with a woman named Susie Pearson.

Susie popped up on my screen, a blueblood for sure, with a perfectly cut blond bob and clad in—of all things!—a cashmere sweater and pearls.

Yay, me! I'd made the right fashion choice.

She appeared to be sitting in a Craftsman bungalow, a massive fireplace in the background.

Too late, I realized that the view behind me was my cramped galley kitchen. I only hoped Susie didn't notice the jar of strawberry jam and cinnamon raisin bagel crumbs on the counter.

We'd barely said our hellos when Prozac came bounding over to join us.

That cat can ignore me for hours on end, but the minute I'm on the phone or Zoom, she's got her little pink nose in my face.

This time, however, she had her tush in my face, hogging the camera.

Pawing at Susie on my computer screen, she gave a friendly meow.

Hi, I'm Prozac! And you are?

"Prozac, get down," I said, plopping her back on the floor.

But she jumped right back up again, meowing at Susie.

Jaine's been taking me for walks, and everybody on the block thinks I'm adorable! What do you think? Adorable, right?

Once again, I pried her away from the screen.

"So sorry about that," I said, holding Prozac firmly in my lap so she couldn't escape.

"That's perfectly all right," Susie said.

But from the stiff smile on her face, I got the feeling it was far from perfectly all right.

Then, in a stroke of good luck, I saw a package of Prozac's kitty treats on the table. I grabbed some and tossed them clear across the room.

Prozac wriggled out of my grasp and jumped back up in front of the camera, with one last meow for Susie.

Nice chatting. Gotta run.

And she was off like a shot to suck up her treats. I feared that the minute she'd scarfed them down, she'd come back for more, but much to my relief, she wandered off down the hallway toward my bedroom.

"Alone at last, haha," I said.

Susie chose to ignore my feeble attempt at humor.

"So, Jaine," she said, "even though you've had no experience in the nonprofit area, the hiring committee liked your writing samples. Confidentially, my husband and I own a Toiletmasters double-flush commode, and we love it!"

At long last, she graced me with a genuine smile, then proceeded to talk about the historical society's mission of preserving Pasadena's grand old houses.

"They were built back when the world was a civilized place," she said wistfully. "Back when people valued tradition, good manners, and old-fashioned values.

"Not like today," she frowned, shaking her perfectly coiffed bob, "where the world has gone to pot. Why, just last night, I saw a woman in jeans at the opera!"

"Some people have no sense of propriety!" I said, pretending to be horrified.

"So tell me," Susie asked, "why you're interested in working for us."

To fulfill my lifelong dream of a steady paycheck was what first popped into my head, but I wisely kept that thought to myself. Instead, I told her about my fascination with old houses, how I loved to tour them and picture myself living in them back when they were first built.

And it's the truth. I really do get off on that stuff.

I guess Susie could hear the fervor in my voice.

"You're exactly the kind of candidate we're looking for," she beamed.

Yes! She liked me!

At that moment, just when everything was going so well, I happened to glance over at the top shelf of my bookcase and gulped in dismay. Prozac had returned from my bedroom and was perched next to my philodendron plant, crouched and poised to attack.

For some reason, she's always had it in for my philoden-dron and periodically takes great pleasure in knocking it to the ground, its pot usually shattering with a godawful crash.

The gleam in her eye told me she was about to strike once again.

"So," Susie was saying, "is there anything else you'd like to tell me?"

"Phooey! Rats! Darn it!"

(Only the expletives I used were a tad more colorful.)

Leaping up from my seat, I dashed to my bookcase, snatching Pro away from the philodendron before she had a chance to send it hurtling to the ground.

It was only when I was returning to my desk that I real-ized that by leaping up, I'd treated Susie to an up-close and personal view of my kittens-in-teacups pajama bot-toms. Which, by the way, were sporting a few well-placed ketchup stains.

Damn it all. I'd just become one of the philistines who wore jeans to the opera.

"My apologies," I said, returning to Susie with Pro in my arms. "My cat was about to knock a plant down from my book case. And excuse the pajama bottoms. They're so very inappropriate for a job interview."

I girded my loins, waiting for a frosty reply from Susie, but much to my surprise, she grinned.

"No worries," she said.

Then she stood up, revealing pajama bottoms covered with Scottie dogs.

"I'm a dog person myself."

Hallelujah! I still had a shot at this prestigious gig.

"I need to talk to the rest of the committee, but I've got a good feeling about you, Jaine. I'll definitely be in touch."

On that encouraging note, our chat closed out, and I whirled around the room, Prozac still in my arms.

"In spite of your best efforts to sabotage the interview, Susie liked me!"

A dismissive yawn from Pro.

But I'm pretty sure she liked me better.

Chapter Nine

Having hacked most of Misty's speeches to words of three syllables or less, I continued showing up at rehearsals, ostensibly to fix the jokes that weren't working (in other words, all of them). But every time I pitched a joke to David, he shot it down.

And Misty was no help, feeding David's already inflated ego.

"Your jokes are so much funnier than Jaine's!" she'd assure him.

Oh, well. Who cared? With any luck, I'd soon be writing copy for the Pasadena Historical Society.

About a week after the infamous morale-boosting dinner, I showed up at the theater to face another round of rejected jokes, armed with a meatball sub I'd picked up at a nearby deli. I'd been bringing in my lunch all week, unwilling to eat one more sproutfest from The Happy Veggie.

On my way in, I bumped into Becca, who was on her way out.

"You leaving" I asked.

"I've got a dentist appointment this morning," she nodded. "Then I've got to pick up that area rug David wants for the living room set. Finally, I've got to head out to

Burbank to rent costumes. I'll probably be gone most of the day."

Lucky Becca, I thought wistfully, watching her slip out the door, wishing I, too, had an excuse to escape Zombieland.

Sitting up front in the audience were Delia and Preston, drinking coffee and chatting. Preston was doing a great job as Vern Abercrombie, trying his best to inject some zest into David's lifeless dialogue. He and Delia had become buddies, swapping theater stories and trashing Misty.

I headed for the kitchen to put my meatball sub in the fridge, and as I passed them, I heard Preston say, "Whose turn is it to spit in Craptessa's smoothie today?"

"Aidan's."

"Lucky devil."

They chuckled heartily, waving hello as I walked by.

Backstage in the kitchen, I stowed my sub in the fridge, then peeked into the pastry box on the kitchen counter. I did this every day, hoping a box of cheese Danishes would miraculously appear. But all I ever saw were those petrified bran muffins. I trolled the cupboards for a mid-morning snack, but found nothing except for some plastic forks and a box of rat poison Becca had bought to deal with the mice crisis.

Why did I get the feeling that even the rat poison would be tastier than those muffins?

I'd just stepped out of the kitchen when I heard Misty's voice coming from the prop area behind the stage, breathless and steamy-sexy.

"Babe," she was cooing, "you are so hot!"

What utter bilge. The new, improved David was lukewarm at best.

"The hottest guy I've ever met," she continued to gush.

Yuck! Was David really falling for this pap?

I tiptoed over to get a better look.

And when I did, I was gobsmacked to see that the object of Misty's lust was not David—but Aidan.

"I'm so sick of faking it with David," she groaned, throwing her arms around Aidan's neck. "Trust me," she added, "I won't be faking it with you!"

"Sorry, Misty." Aidan wrenched free from her embrace. "Wrong team."

"What do you mean?"

"I'm gay."

"That's okay," Misty replied with a wink. "I like a challenge."

What an ego. What play did she think she was starring in anyway? *The Miracle Worker*?

"C'mon," she said, opening a trapdoor in the floor. "Let's go down to the cellar for some private fun and games. David and I go there all the time. You'll like it. And I promise you won't be gay when I'm through with you."

Unwilling to watch one more minute of this nonsense, I turned to leave.

And that's when I realized I was not alone.

Standing behind me was David, rigid with rage.

That day everything changed—starting with our lunch orders.

"I'm sick of The Happy Veggie," David said. "Today we're ordering from Fatburger."

Yes!!

"But what about my smoothie?" Misty pouted.

"Order it yourself," David snapped. "I'm not paying for it anymore."

Misty blinked in confusion.

"I don't understand. I thought you liked vegan food."

"No, Misty. I was just faking it. You know all about faking it, don't you?"

A bright red flush suffused Misty's face as she no doubt realized David must have seen her flirting with Aidan.

But apparently she decided to play it wide-eyed and innocent.

"David, what's wrong?"

"Nothing's wrong. Nothing at all. Except for your performance. Try to put a little life in it today, okay?"

And so it went through the morning's rehearsal—David trashing Misty, calling out her every mistake, and lavishing praise on the other actors.

At one point, he grabbed Misty's cell phone from her when, during one of Delia's speeches, she took it out and checked the screen.

"Give me that!" he said. "Show the other actors the common courtesy of paying attention when they're speaking."

Then he glanced down at her phone, shaking his head in disgust at what he saw.

"Jaine," he called out to me, "take this and put it in Misty's dressing room."

I hustled up to the stage and took the phone from David, then headed off backstage. I was dying to look at Misty's phone and see what had triggered David's disgust. But that would be snooping. And that would be wrong.

So of course, I went ahead and took a peek.

Unfortunately, David had clicked off the phone, and I needed a passcode to get in. I took a wild guess and punched in the one passcode I figured Misty was capable of remembering: One-two-three-four.

Bingo! It worked.

I scanned her most recent texts, but all I saw was a thread about a sale at an establishment called Naughty Nighties.

Then I tried her photos and hit pay dirt.

There on the screen was a selfie of Misty in bed with a mystery man.

Egotist that she was, her body took up most of the photo. The only visible part of her lover was his ankle, tattooed with a snake.

By now, I'd reached the door to Misty's dressing room, where, in happier days, David had hung a gold star. Inside, I saw a large couch, adorned with lip-shaped throw pillows—the love nest where David's "coaching" sessions must have taken place.

I put the phone on a nearby vanity table and headed out to join the others.

Back onstage, they'd reached the end of Act One, where Misty and David kiss. Up until then, the torrid duo had tackled their smooching with gusto. But there was no locking lips that day—David holding Misty at arm's length.

"Aren't we supposed to kiss here?" Misty asked.

"Let's save it for opening night. You've played enough love scenes for one morning."

By now, Misty couldn't ignore it any longer. David had caught her coming on to Aidan, and she needed to appease him somehow.

"Look, David," she said, "if you overheard me and Aidan earlier, it wasn't for real. I was just helping him run lines for another play. Right, Aidan?"

"Um . . . uh," Aidan stammered, looking like he wished he could drop through that trapdoor to the cellar.

Luckily, he didn't have to answer the question, because just then two delivery guys showed up—one with lunch from Fatburger, the other with Misty's lunch and her beloved smoothie.

Eager to escape, Aidan hustled off to put Misty's smoothie in the fridge.

Misty, looking more than a tad desperate, batted her eyes at David, asking, "Aren't you going to come with me to my dressing room to run lines?"

David just glared at her.

"Run your own lines. And this time, make sure you remember them."

Misty wandered off, dazed, to her dressing room.

The other actors were a bit dazed, too, clearly wondering what had caused this seismic shift in David, from besotted lover to acerbic critic.

Whatever the reason, Delia was particularly overjoyed, practically purring with glee.

"C'mon, Delia," David said. "Let's you and I have lunch together. I want to hear all about your days working on Broadway."

They sat next to each other in the audience, Delia regaling David with show biz gossip. On the other side of the aisle, Aidan shared lunch with Preston, who was no doubt pressing Aidan for details about what had gone on between him and Misty.

I sat several rows behind the others, working on the script. David had instructed me to cut Misty's speeches wherever possible.

"And I may have been too hasty rejecting some of your jokes," he said. "Put them back if you think they're funny."

I went to work, pruning Misty's speeches, adding jokes, and scarfing down my Fatburger, which, I must say, was dee-lish. I couldn't resist ordering one, along with a side of fries, figuring I'd have my meatball sub for dinner that night.

Every once in a while. I heard peals of laughter from Delia and David, but I was so engrossed in my work, I wasn't really paying attention to the others.

That is, until I ran out of ketchup for my fries. Major emergency. So I scooted off to the kitchen to hunt for stray ketchup packets.

Misty's dressing room door was open when I got backstage, and I could hear her on the phone with what appeared to be her former restaurant manager, telling him she might soon be available to work the dinner shift. She must've realized her cruise on the SS *Cryptessa* was possibly coasting to an end.

In the kitchen, I managed to find a lone ketchup packet in one of the cupboards. Once again, I peeked into the pastry box, still hoping for a miracle Danish, but naturally, that wish didn't come true.

Just as I was leaving the kitchen, the theater's rusty side door screeched open and a bald guy in a HYDREX EXTERMINATORS work shirt showed up with some mousetraps.

At last, the landlord had sent someone to take care of the mice. And the most annoying pest on the premises, Misty, had just been royally zapped by David.

What a pleasant day this was turning out to be.

Rehearsals resumed after lunch.

For once, Misty was trying her best to inject some life into her lines, but David kept reaming into her anyway.

Then, desperate to please, Misty said, "I know all the words to my song, David. I've been rehearsing all during lunch."

The song to which Misty referred was the one I'd heard the day of my interview, belted out by the other, far more talented actress.

In case you've forgotten (and who can blame you?), it was the little ditty where Cryptessa sang those immortal words:

Even though I was undead I couldn't bear to stay unwed and *Who would have thought a zombie would wind up as Mrs. Brad Abercrombie?*

Throughout the rehearsals, the song had been a bone of contention between Becca and David, Becca convinced Misty would never remember so many lines at once, David insisting that she would.

And it looked like David was right.

That day, Misty sang every single word of the song.

All of them, unfortunately, off key.

When she was through, David sighed and hollered out to me, "Jaine, rewrite the lyrics so Delia can sing it."

Misty gulped, crushed.

Rehearsals continued, with David giving Misty the deep freeze.

Then three o'clock rolled around. Normally everything ground to a halt while Misty sucked down her smoothie.

But David just kept going.

Finally, when they'd reached the end of the scene they'd been working on, Misty asked meekly, "Is it okay if I have my smoothie now?"

"What the hell?" David said. "Have your stupid smoothie. We could use a break anyway. Take five, everybody."

"I'll get it," Aidan said, starting for the kitchen as he did every day.

"Aidan, you don't have to bring Misty her smoothie," David said. "If she wants it, she can get it herself."

"I don't mind," Aidan said, hurrying off.

It was possible he wanted to get the smoothie so he could spit in it. After all, it was his turn. But I didn't think so. He looked like he actually felt sorry for Misty. And by now, I couldn't help but feel a wee bit sorry for her myself.

Minutes later, Aidan was back with Misty's green goop.

He handed it to her, and for the first time in my recollection, I heard her say the words "Thank you."

We usually just sat around and watched her drink it, but that day David was chatting it up with Delia and Preston, pointedly ignoring his ingenue.

Alone and dejected, Misty took a few sips.

"This smoothie tastes funny," she said, wrinkling her nose.

"Just drink the damn thing," David snapped, "so we can get back to rehearsal."

Reluctantly Misty took a few more swallows.

"I'm done," she said, finally.

Prophetic words, indeed.

Because just then, she doubled over, writhing in pain. The most energetic performance she'd given to date.

But this was no performance. This was real. By now she'd collapsed onto the floor.

"Somebody call nine-one-one!" Delia cried.

I made the call, but it was too late.

By the time the paramedics showed up, Misty had gone from undead to just plain dead.

Chapter Ten

In no time, the theater was swarming with police hovering over Misty's corpse.

"Who's in charge here?" asked a barrel-chested cop whose name tag read M. SANTIAGO.

"Um . . . I am," David said groggily, as if waking from a trance.

"Can you tell me what happened?" M. Santiago asked.

But David just stood there, speechless. So Delia took over, explaining how Misty had been drinking her smoothie when she suddenly doubled over in pain and collapsed.

"You all need to clear the stage," M. Santiago said when Delia had finished her recap of events, "and wait for the homicide detective to show up and question you."

"Question us? Surely you can't suspect any of us of murder!" Delia said, drawing herself up to her full height, the outraged grand dame.

"The very idea is preposterous!" Preston chimed in.

"Just clear the stage," M. Santiago repeated, "and wait until you're told to go."

As we stepped down into the audience, I could hear one of the cops saying, "We found rat poison in the kitchen. That's probably what did her in."

Unlike the others, I had no trouble whatsoever believing

Misty had been murdered. Selfish, arrogant, and manipulative, the woman practically had a "kill me" bull's-eye pinned on her back.

And I was pretty certain I knew who did it: David.

No matter how much the other actors disliked Misty, it was hard to believe they'd go so far as to kill her. Besides, she'd already gotten her comeuppance from David that day. She'd been humiliated in front of all of us, payback for all the bad karma she'd been tossing our way, her co-stars lapping up every minute of it.

David was the one who'd been betrayed and enraged. He'd even bullied Misty into drinking more of her smoothie. Maybe she'd still be alive if she hadn't taken those few extra sips.

"This play has been a disaster from the get-go," Delia was saying as I joined her, Preston, and Aidan in the audience. "First having to act with the little brat and now practically being accused of her murder. I can just see my future job offers going up in flames."

"I can't believe one of us offed her," Preston said.

"Actually, I can." Delia looked over at David, who'd chosen to sit alone across the aisle, staring out into space. "David was lashing out at Misty all day," she said, voicing my thoughts aloud. "He sure looked like he wanted to kill her."

"I wonder what that was all about," Preston said.

"I have a pretty good idea." Aidan sighed. "Misty was coming on to me this morning, dissing David and throwing herself at me. I guess David must have seen us."

"He did," I piped up. "I was there, too."

"I just hope the police don't think I did it," Aidan groaned. "I was the one who brought Misty her smoothie. If only I'd let her get it herself!"

"Don't worry," said Delia, patting his arm. "Just because you were the one who brought her the smoothie doesn't mean you killed her."

How true. Any one of them could have slipped into the kitchen during lunch break and tossed a fatal dose of rat poison into her drink.

But my money was still on David.

The homicide detective showed up just then, a no-nonsense brunette in a polyester pant suit, her hair scraped back into a tight ponytail. Soon she'd set up headquarters in Preston's dressing room and was calling us, one by one, to be questioned.

Aidan was summoned first, and from the ashen look on his face when he came back, it seemed as if his earlier fears may have been justified.

"How'd it go?" Preston asked.

"Not great," Aidan mumbled, distraught, as he hurried past us out of the theater.

When Delia was summoned next, Preston excused himself to call his wife, moving several rows behind me.

I sneaked another glance at David, who was still sitting, dazed and glassy-eyed—like a man who, in a moment of rage, had poisoned his lover's smoothie and was just now beginning to realize the enormity of what he'd done.

I thought about how happy he must have been months ago when he won that lottery money, and how miserable he was now. They say lottery winners often wind up worse than when they started out, that it's more often a curse than a blessing. It sure seemed true for David. If he'd never won that money, he'd never have produced his play and gotten mixed up with Misty.

I was ruminating on life's ironic twists, the vagaries of fate, and what to get for dinner when I remembered the meatball sub I'd stowed in the fridge. It had been a while since lunch, and by now, I was feeling quite peckish.

That meatball sub would sure hit the spot.

Up onstage, the police were busy taking pictures of Misty's body and bagging her smoothie. They seemed pretty engrossed in their work, so I took a chance and managed to slip past them and go backstage. There I made a beeline for the kitchen, my mouth watering at the thought of my meatball sub.

So you can imagine my disappointment when I saw a CRIME SCENE DO NOT CROSS tape strung across the kitchen entrance.

Phooey! I wanted my sub!

Surely, it wouldn't matter if I popped over to the fridge and got it.

I ducked under the tape and was just retrieving my meatball masterpiece when I heard:

"What do you think you're doing?"

I looked up and saw M. Santiago glaring at me.

"I was just getting my meatball sub," I said, ducking back out from under the tape.

"What you're doing is tampering with a crime scene," he said, whipping my beloved sandwich away from me.

Why did I get the feeling he was going to be chowing down on it the minute I was out of sight?

"You Jaine Austen?" he asked.

"Yes," I said, my eyes still riveted on my sub. "That's me."

"You're up next. Detective Jamison will see you now."

With my sub clutched in his hand, he led me to Preston's dressing room, where Detective Jamison was sitting at Preston's vanity table.

"Have a seat, Ms. Austen," she said, gesturing to a rumpsprung armchair.

I plopped down across from the no-frills, sharp-eyed detective.

From the bulging muscles on her thighs, it looked like she might have been a spin class instructor in a former life.

"I caught her in the kitchen," M. Santiago said, ratting me out. "She claims she was looking for this."

He waved the plastic deli carton containing my meatball sub.

"That'll be all, sergeant," the detective said, dismissing her underling. "I'll take it from here."

As he lumbered out the door, Jamison turned to me and got straight to the point.

"Do you have any idea who might have killed Misty Baines?"

"Actually, I do."

But before I could share my thoughts, her cell phone rang.

"Excuse me," she said, taking it out of her pocket and glancing at it. "I've got to take this.

"How many times have I told you not to call me when I'm working?" she hissed to her caller. "This better be an emergency. So what's up? . . . You forgot them again?" She shook her ponytail, exasperated. "Just look under the flower pot. There's always a spare key there."

She hung up with a sigh.

"My son. Locked himself out of the house again." Then, no doubt remembering she was supposed to be investigating a homicide, she asked, "So where were we?

"You asked me if I knew who killed Misty."

"Right."

Once again, her cell phone dinged just as I was about to solve the murder.

"Sorry," she mouthed at me, taking the call. "What do you mean it's not under the flowerpot? It's always under the flower pot . . . Okay, then just let yourself in through the kitchen window. It's unlocked."

She clicked off her phone, and I finally got to tell her how David had fallen for Misty, how crazy he'd been about her, and how that very morning, he'd seen her cheating on him and coming on to Aidan.

"He was beyond furious with Misty," I said.

"Furious enough to kill her?"

"I think so."

"It says here," she said, consulting her notes, "that you're a writer."

Oh, dear. I didn't like the spotlight suddenly shining on me.

"Yes. I don't usually write plays, though. Usually I write toilet bowl ads. For Toiletmasters Plumbers. *In a Rush to Flush? Call Toiletmasters!* I wrote that. Won the Golden Plunger Award from the Los Angeles Plumbers' Association. But I'm trying to branch out to the theater. I'm also up for a job writing press releases for the Pasadena Historical Society. Fingers crossed I get it!"

I tend to babble when I'm nervous.

"According to my notes," Detective Jamison said, "it appears that the victim had been known to make disparaging remarks about your jokes."

Who the heck threw me under the bus? I wondered, most annoyed.

"True," I said, "but Misty trashed everybody."

"You sure you weren't harboring any resentment toward the deceased?"

"Not enough to kill her!"

My vehement denial was cut off, however, when once again her phone rang.

"What now?" she snapped, taking the call. ". . . You broke into Mr. Engel's house by mistake? How the heck can you not recognize your own house?"

I spent the next few minutes listening to her apologize profusely to her irate neighbor.

Then she hung up with a sigh.

"You got any teenagers?" she wanted to know.

"Nope."

"Want one?" she asked. "Only kidding," she added. "Sort of."

She dismissed me then, and I left her back on her phone, begging Mr. Engel not to press charges against her doofus son.

Out in the audience, Becca had returned from her errands and was at David's side, holding his hand.

"Don't worry, honey," I heard her say. "Everything's going to be okay."

Don't bet the rent on it, I felt like telling them.

I just hoped David had enough money left over from his lottery winnings to hire himself a good attorney.

Slinging my purse over my shoulder, I started outside, pretty sure David was the killer, and certain that M. Santiago was somewhere in the theater scarfing down my meatball sub.

You've Got Mail

To: Jausten
From: DaddyO
Subject: Banished!

Your mom's book club ladies are coming for lunch today, and, as usual, I've been banished from the premises. (I don't care what Mom says; I still think the ladies like it when I entertain them with my repertoire of Henny Youngman jokes.)

Oh, well. I don't mind. The last thing I want is to run into the Battle Axe, who rules that club with an iron fist. Why Mom joined in the first place is a mystery to me. She reads romance novels by the dozen, but hardly ever makes it past the first chapter in the "classic" books Lydia assigns.

Mom made me lock Iggy in his cage in the guest bedroom. I hated to do it, but it's only for a few hours. I'll let him loose the minute I come home.

Meanwhile, I'm off to have lunch with Nick Roulakis at the clubhouse. The poor sap actually thinks he has a snowball's chance in hell of winning first prize in the talent show playing "Lady of Spain" on his harmonica. Hah! No way is anyone going to top the show biz magic of me tap-dancing with an iguana on my head!

Love 'n cuddles from
Daddy
(and Iggy too!)

To: Jausten
From: Shoptillyoudrop
Subject: All Set for Book Club

I'm all set for my book club, sweetheart. Daddy's gone to have lunch with Nick Roulakis, and Iggy is safely locked up in his cage. I spent the morning watching the movie version of *Wuthering Heights* and just finished garnishing my Crab Louis salad, which I'll be serving with croissants and flourless chocolate cake for dessert.

I read somewhere that dark chocolate is a vital source of antioxidants and can lower your risk of heart disease.

I'm choosing to believe it's true.
XOXO,
Mom

To: Jausten
From: DaddyO
Subject: Missing!

Brace yourself for catastrophic news, Lambchop.
Iggy is missing!

When I got home from lunch, I went to the guest bedroom to let Iggy out of his cage, and got the shock of my life to see the door to the cage wide open, Iggy nowhere in sight.

I've searched every square inch of the house and can't find the little fella anywhere.

Someone obviously let him out of his cage. And that someone can be only one person—Lydia Pinkus! The Battle Axe must've heard about my blockbuster tap-dancing routine with Iggy and tossed him out into the wilds of Tampa Vistas in a dastardly attempt to sabotage our act.

Well, she's not going to get away with it! I'm going to comb every square inch of Tampa Vistas until I'm reunited with my reptilian buddy.

Let the search begin!

Love 'n hugs from
Your outraged
Daddy

To: Jausten
From: Shoptillyoudrop
Subject: Utter Nonsense

Oh, my stars. You'd think the world had just stopped spinning on its axis the way your father is carrying on.

Iggy's not in his cage, and we can't find him anywhere. Daddy is convinced Lydia let him loose in the "wilds" of Tampa Vistas to sabotage his act.

Utter nonsense! Yes, it's true Lydia excused herself to use the bathroom during book club, but I can't believe she crept into the guest bedroom, unlocked the cage, scooped Iggy into her arms, and tossed him outside.

I'm sure it's all Daddy's fault. He probably didn't latch the cage door properly, and Iggy wandered out by himself.

Dollars to donuts Iggy's hiding somewhere in the house, just waiting for a chance to dart out of nowhere and scare the stuffing out of me.

XOXO,
Mom

Chapter Eleven

For a gal who'd just witnessed a grisly death by smoothie, I woke up the next morning feeling quite chipper.

First, there was the good news (for once!) from Tampa Vistas. Frankly, I was thrilled to learn that Iggy was missing. I wouldn't have been at all surprised if he'd plotted his own escape, dreading the thought of being Daddy's top-hatted partner at the talent show.

As for Misty, I was sorry she was dead. But I certainly wasn't going to miss her. I doubted anyone on the planet—aside from her parents—would. And even her parents seemed like an iffy bet. I could just picture Misty storming out on them with nary a hug goodbye the minute she turned eighteen.

Yes, I was in fine fettle that morning, thinking how wonderful it would be if David and Becca shut down production of *I Married a Zombie* now that they'd lost their leading lady. I'd had more than my share of rewrites and would be a happy camper indeed if I'd seen the last of what had to be the worst play ever written.

And so I tootled off to the kitchen with hope in my heart and tiny bits of pretzels in my hair (a souvenir of a late-night pretzels 'n ice cream binge).

After fixing Prozac a bowl of Hearty Halibut Innards, I

nuked myself coffee and a cinnamon raisin bagel. I'd just taken the bagel out of the microwave when the phone rang.

I hurried to get it, hoping it was Becca telling me the final curtain had rung on *I Married a Zombie*.

But it wasn't Becca. It was a guy named Brandon.

"I'm Skyler McEnroe's personal assistant," he explained.

"Skyler who?"

"Skyler McEnroe, the bachelor you bid on at the Gwyneth Paltrow School of Organic Cosmetology auction."

Oh, right. My chipper mood vanished when I remembered the six hundred bucks I'd spent for a date with a slick entrepreneur and patron of the arts.

"Mr. McEnroe is wondering if you'd be free on Friday for dinner?"

"Um. Sure," I said, hoping I wasn't supposed to pick up the tab.

Six hundred smackeroos were the absolute maximum I intended to fork over to the Gwyneth Paltrow School of Organic Cosmetology.

"Great," Brandon said. "Mr. McEnroe will call for you at six."

I hung up, certain that Skyler McEnroe never dated anyone outside the model/actress/call girl demographic favored by L.A.'s mega-rich guys. In fact, I bet my bottom Pop-Tart I'd be the first woman ever to show up for a date with Skyler McEnroe with elastic in her waistband and cellulite on her thighs.

Which reminded me, I was all out of Pop-Tarts. I made a mental note to stock up ASAP.

Back in the kitchen, I finished prepping my bagel, slathering it, as always, with gobs of butter and strawberry jam. And I was just settling on my sofa to scarf it down when Lance came banging at my front door.

Why does that man always show up just when I'm about to dig into a cinnamon raisin bagel?

With a sigh, I got up and opened the door to find Lance looking drawn and haggard, having abandoned his usual fashion-plate look for tattered jeans and a baggy tee.

"Horrible news," he groaned, slumping down onto my sofa.

Sensing his distress, Prozac leaped down from the armchair where she'd been belching hearty halibut fumes and hurried over to his lap to comfort him.

"The actress who played Cryptessa was murdered yesterday. And the police think Aidan did it! Just because he brought her a smoothie."

"Don't panic, Lance. The police are questioning everybody. The detective in charge of the case even hinted that I might have done it."

"Really?" he asked, a glimmer of hope in his eyes.

"You needn't look so happy about it."

"Of course I'm not happy about it, Jaine. But better you than Aidan."

No, he didn't say that last part. But I had a sneaky suspicion he was thinking it.

"They can't convict Aidan just because he was the one who brought Misty the smoothie," I pointed out. "Anyone could have tampered with it."

"But they took him in to be fingerprinted, and it turns out his prints are all over the box of rat poison that killed her."

"They are?"

"Yes, but only because it was Aidan's job to sprinkle the stuff on the baseboards," he sighed, slumping down even lower on the sofa. "Just my rotten luck," he said. "I finally meet the love of my life, and now he's about to be arrested!"

Prozac, who'd been nuzzling him in that comforting way she has with anyone but me, jerked to attention.

Wait! What? I thought I was the love of your life.

With that, she jumped off his lap, indignant, and scampered back to the armchair, where she promptly proceeded to give herself a thorough gynecological exam.

Lance turned to me, desperate.

"You've got to do your Sherlock Holmes bit, Jaine, and prove Aidan is innocent."

The Sherlock Holmes bit to which he referred is my penchant for tracking down killers. I'm really quite good at it, if I do say so myself.

"Of course I'll help," I assured him.

"Thank you, hon, from the bottom of my heart," Lance said, misty-eyed with gratitude. "Ever since Aidan told me the bad news, I've been a total wreck. I barely slept a wink and can't eat a thing."

That last part he said while reaching for half of my cinnamon raisin bagel.

"Can't eat a thing, huh?" I asked, eyeing the bagel en route to his mouth.

"Okay, so I've managed to choke down a few morsels. But everything tastes like cardboard. Got any grape jelly?"

I shuffled off to the kitchen to get Lance his grape jelly. When I got back, I found him checking his phone.

"What do you think?" he asked, holding out the screen. "I just got a 'like' from this guy."

I looked down at a photo of a handsome honey on one of Lance's many dating apps.

"What the heck are you doing on Tinder? What happened to Aidan, the love of your life?"

"I've got to face facts, Jaine. Aidan could be arrested any minute. What if they find him guilty and send him to jail? Yes, he's my one true love, and I'd visit him in the slammer every week, but I've got to have a plan B in place just in case."

"A plan B?" I cried, giving him the absolute stinkiest of stink eyes.

He had the good grace to look abashed.

"You're right," he said, clicking off his phone. "It's too soon to work on plan B. I'm ashamed of myself for even going there."

And so he headed out the door, ashamed—but not too ashamed to be munching on the other half of my bagel.

Chapter Twelve

Becca called the next day, bubbling over with excitement.

"Great news, Jaine! We've got a fantastic actress to play the part of Cryptessa, and the police have given us the okay to return to the theater. We're going back to the original script, and I need you to come to rehearsals tomorrow to look for cuts and punch-ups."

Oh, groan. Back to square one.

It looked like my stint in the land of the undead would never end.

When I showed up at the theater the next day, Becca came hurrying over to greet me with a cute young blonde in tow.

"Jaine," she beamed, "meet Katie Gustafson, our new Cryptessa!"

"Hi, there!" Katie said with a friendly grin. Something I never once got from Misty.

I recognized her right away as the same dynamo I'd seen auditioning the day of my interview. With her blunt-cut blond bob, big blue eyes, and fresh-scrubbed complexion, she was the perfect girl next door.

Or, in this case, zombie next door.

"So nice to meet you," I said.

"Likewise. Becca tells me you're terrific!"

My, this was turning out to be quite the love fest. Maybe my return to *I Married a Zombie* wasn't going to be so bad after all.

I wandered backstage to the kitchen to pour myself a cup of coffee and was thrilled to discover that Misty's ghastly petrified muffins had been banished, replaced by a box of plump Danish pastries. I chose a cheese beauty, drizzled with icing.

Yes, indeedie. Things were looking up in zombieland.

Once the other actors had shown up and been introduced to Katie, rehearsals began. None of us knew it then, but a seismic change was about to take place.

Katie was everything Misty wasn't—bright, sharp, and funny—a positively enchanting Cryptessa.

The other actors were clearly energized by her, their performances livelier than I'd ever seen them. Even Aidan, in spite of his recent unsettling chat with the police, seemed to be enjoying himself as zany Uncle Dedly.

Becca watched from the audience, beaming.

The only one not caught up in the excitement was David.

Gone were his aviators and tight jeans; he was back in his dweeb duds: muddy brown corduroys and a faded *Star Wars* tee.

Not only was he practically sleepwalking through his performance as Brad Abercrombie, he seemed to have lost all interest in directing. Up until then, he'd been a constant source of bad acting advice.

Now he was silent as one of the prop tombstones.

Instead, Becca seemed to have taken over the reins as director, occasionally offering her advice, but mostly buoying her actors with praise.

I sat at her side, looking for places to make cuts. (I still thought the whole play could be tossed in the shredder with no discernible loss, but thanks to Katie and the others, David's clunky dialogue was actually coming to life.)

Every once in a while, Becca whispered rewrite suggestions to me, most of them pretty darn good. Her creative instincts, formerly stifled as David's assistant, were now in full bloom, and the rehearsal sailed along seamlessly.

When it was time for lunch, we ordered from Fatburger. I was in chowhound heaven.

Best news yet, the exterminator's traps seemed to be working. There wasn't a mouse in sight.

And with Misty gone, we'd gotten rid of our rat problem, too.

I ate lunch onstage with the actors, while out in the audience, Becca and David sat together, shoulders touching, talking softly. Whatever rift Misty had caused between them seemed to have been healed.

Up onstage, Delia, Preston, and Katie ate their lunch on the set's living room sofa, while Aidan and I shared an ottoman.

"I can't tell you how happy we are to have you on board," Delia was telling Katie.

"I can't tell you how happy I am to be here," our new ingenue replied. "It's been almost a year since I moved from Minneapolis, and I was beginning to think I was never going to land a part."

Then her smile faded.

"I'm just sorry I got hired because the other actress was murdered. It's all so tragic."

"Not really," Delia said, popping a fry in her mouth. "I think humanity will survive quite nicely without Misty."

"Delia!" Preston chided. "That's pretty harsh."

"C'mon," Delia replied. "We all hated her. I know you're

not supposed to speak ill of the dead, but in Misty's case, I'm willing to make an exception."

"She really was bad news," Aidan agreed.

"At any rate, we're glad you're here," Preston said to Katie. "I thought for sure the play would close opening night, but now, who knows? Maybe we've got a shot."

"Maybe we do," Delia said. "The play's so bad, it just might be good."

"It could be a camp classic!" Aidan chimed in.

The actors continued to chat about the play with mounting enthusiasm, every once in a while tossing in a horror story about Misty.

I contributed nothing to the conversation, too busy inhaling my fatburger.

When it was almost time to resume rehearsals and the others had scattered off backstage to make phone calls or hit the restroom, I took Aidan aside.

"So how are you holding up?"

"Fine!" he assured me with a bright smile.

"Really?"

"Okay, maybe not so fine," he conceded. "I told the police the only reason my fingerprints were on the box of rat poison was because I was in charge of sprinkling the stuff on the baseboards, but I could tell I'm still not out from under their radar. When the detective in charge of the case found out how Misty came on to me, she hinted that I might have killed her in a 'Me Too' moment of rage. It's nuts, of course," he said, dismissing Detective Jamison's theory with a wave of his hand.

But I could see the fear in his eyes.

"Actually," I said, "I've solved a couple of murders in the past."

"I know. Lance told me. Your track record is very impressive."

"And I'd be glad to do some snooping for you, if you'd like."

"Would you?" he said eagerly. "That'd be great!"

"Did you happen to notice anyone going backstage during lunch break the day of the murder?" I asked, switching to part-time semi-professional PI mode.

"Only Preston. We'd been eating lunch together, and he excused himself to go to his dressing room to call his agent. But I have a hard time believing he killed Misty. He barely knew her."

I agreed. I couldn't see Preston as the killer, either.

There was only one person who hated Misty enough to spike her smoothie with rat poison, the guy who'd fallen head over heels in love with her, only to discover she was a user and a cheat.

Nope, in this homicide horse race, my money was still on David.

Chapter Thirteen

Misty's murder was on the back burner of my brain that night as I sat at Paco's Tacos, sipping a margarita and inhaling tortilla chips, waiting for Kandi to join me for dinner. Listening to the faint whir of the margarita blender and breathing in the enticing aroma of sizzling steak fajitas, I was soon lulled into a dreamlike state, lost in a rather naughty fantasy featuring me, Jude Law, and a vat of guacamole.

I was stirred from my X-rated reverie when Kandi came rushing over to our table, looking more than a tad frazzled.

"What a day!" she said, plopping down across from me, raking her hair from her forehead. I couldn't help but notice that, even in her distress, her chestnut bob was as shiny as ever.

"Trouble on the set? "

"Big trouble. The day after the cockroach gets out of rehab, Tommy the Termite gets arrested on a DUI. I swear, it's like our show has been sprayed by a karmic can of Raid."

For the first time, she noticed the margarita I'd ordered for her and took a grateful sip.

Needless to say, my size-6 friend didn't even think about

reaching for a chip. Which was a good thing, since I'd finished them all.

"But look who I'm talking to about trouble on the job," Kandi said. "I read about the actress from your play getting murdered."

"It was pretty awful. And the police think that Lance's friend Aidan may have done it. Lance is going nuts, and I don't blame him. Aidan's a really sweet guy."

Kandi's eyes widened in alarm.

"Please don't tell me you're going to go racing off on some crazy mission to find the killer!"

"Of course not," I fibbed, eager to avoid a lecture on the dangers of tracking down homicidal maniacs.

When our waiter showed up to take our orders, we did our usual thing: tostada salad for Kandi, chicken chimichangas for me.

"Guess what?" Kandi said when he'd gone. "In all the hoo-ha of Tommy the Termite's DUI, I forgot to tell you. I had a date with Ethan, my yachtsman."

"How was it?"

"Divine! His boat is in dry dock, getting repainted. But he took me to dinner at his yacht club. We sat at a table out on the deck with a fantastic view of the marina, where we watched the sunset with oysters and champagne, and the moonrise with lobster and chardonnay.

"It was positively magical!" she gushed, her eyes aglow at the memory.

"And it turns out we both love mountain biking, Marvel action movies, and pineapple on our pizza."

"Kandi, you don't like any of those things."

"Not yet. But I'm sure I will, once I try them. Anything will be fun with a guy as special as Ethan. You should see his eyes. They're the exact same turquoise as a Tiffany box!"

Her ode to Ethan was interrupted just then by the sound of her cell phone pinging.

"That's probably him!" she squealed in delight. "Do you mind if I get it?"

"Go for it."

But the minute she checked her cell, her smile vanished.

"It's a text from Tommy the Termite. They've suspended his driver's license. Now we're going to have to hire a car service to take him to and from the studio every day."

She clicked off her phone with a groan.

"So what about you?" she asked, no doubt eager to distract herself from her termite woes. "What's up with you and your bachelor?"

"I haven't met him yet. He's taking me out for dinner on Friday."

"Oh, goodie!" she cried. "I'm so excited for you!"

"Don't be. I doubt I'll have anything in common with a bizguy entrepreneur."

"You've got to think positive, Jaine! Imagine yourself going out on a fantastic date. Remember what I told you about visualization? If you picture what you want, it will come to you. It really works!"

"Maybe you're right," I said as the chimichangas I'd been visualizing for the past fifteen minutes showed up at the table. Did I mention they came smothered in sour cream and guacamole?

"Why, only yesterday," Kandi was saying, oblivious to her tostada salad, "I bought the cutest bikini to wear on Ethan's sailboat. Just visualizing myself there will make it happen."

It shows what good friends we are that I didn't hate Kandi for being able to try on bathing suits without the aid of intravenous tranquilizers.

I must confess, though, that I sort of tuned her out as she went on to describe the bikini, as well as Ethan's amazing eyes, winning smile, and sparkling personality. Or maybe it was his sparkling eyes, winning personality, and amazing smile.

Like I said, I was too busy chowing down on my chimichangas to pay attention.

When I finally came up for air, Kandi had returned to the subject of my upcoming bachelor date.

"You've got to promise me that you'll cut out all desserts between now and then."

I knew better than to argue with her.

"I promise," I said, fingers firmly crossed under the table.

"And you must absolutely not stop off at the supermarket on the way home for Chunky Monkey."

"Absolutely not. No way. Never!" I assured her, scraping the last of the sour cream from my plate.

The thing is, I had no intention of stopping off for Chunky Monkey that night. Not until Kandi planted the idea in my head.

Yes, I promised I wouldn't get any, but you should know by now that when it comes to Chunky Monkey, I simply can't be trusted.

So fifteen minutes after I'd hugged Kandi goodbye, I was pulling into the parking lot of my local supermarket for my Chunky Monkey fix. I figured I could burn off some calories trotting from the parking lot to the ice cream aisle.

Which I did, feeling quite noble.

I was just reaching into the freezer case for my chocolate and banana treat when a message came over the PA.

"Attention, shopper Jaine Austen. Your friend Kandi

called to remind you to stay away from the Chunky Monkey. I repeat. Shopper Jaine Austen, stay away from the Chunky Monkey."

I stood there, dumbfounded. I couldn't believe Kandi would sink so low as to rat me out to my supermarket.

But I took her message to heart, and you'll be happy to know that I did not buy any Chunky Monkey that night.

I bought Chocolate Fudge Brownie instead.

Ever vigilant about sticking to my supermarket exercise regimen, I trotted over to the checkout counter and handed my bounty to a rail-thin checker with purple hair and chipped orange nail polish.

She looked at me, then at the ice cream, then back at me again, eyes narrowed like a TSA agent looking for full-size shampoo in a carry-on.

"You're Jaine Austen, aren't you?"

I didn't dignify that with a reply. It was none of her darn beeswax.

"Your friend Kandi told us to be on the lookout for a lady with brown curly hair and a guacamole stain on her blazer."

Damn. I looked down, and, sure enough, there was a guacamole stain on the lapel of my blazer.

"You sure you want this?" My purple-haired inquisitor asked, holding up my ice cream.

"Yes, I'm sure."

"Wouldn't you rather have some rice cakes? They're on sale, half price on aisle twelve."

I had no doubt they were on sale. They had to unload them somehow.

"Sounds mighty tempting, but I'll pass."

"Okay," she shrugged, "but these calories aren't going to work themselves off your hips."

Of all the nerve!

"And that chipped polish isn't going to remove itself from your nails," I countered. "I think I saw nail polish remover on aisle twenty."

That shut her up pretty darn quick.

I'm proud to say I strode out of the supermarket with my head held high, my dignity intact, and a pint of Chocolate Fudge Brownie ice cream in my shopping tote.

(Okay, two pints.)

Chapter Fourteen

They say that a monkey sitting at a typewriter, given an infinite amount of time, would eventually be able to bang out one of Shakespeare's plays. I bet that that same monkey, working with one hand tied behind his back and spending half his days checking his Twitter feed, would be a Tony winner compared to David.

It was déjà vu all over again as I returned to David's original nightmare of a script.

I pretty much made the same cuts I'd already made, punching up what passed for jokes wherever possible. Then I emailed the results to Becca, who called to tell me she was happy with my changes and planned to lock in the script to give the actors a chance to learn their lines.

"So we won't need you at rehearsals," she said.

What blessed news! If I had to take one more pass at that script, I'd go bonkers.

Just as I was about to jump for joy, it occurred to me that if I wasn't at rehearsals, I wouldn't be able to question my suspects.

"Say, Becca," I said, "I've had so much fun working with everyone, it would be great if I had a way to keep in touch."

"No problem. I'll send you a contact list. I'm sure they'd all love to hear from you."

Sure enough, within minutes, she'd emailed me the list.

Time to start snooping.

Springing to action, I made plans to meet Delia for drinks that night at a restaurant near her condo in Westwood. I'd texted her, telling her I had something important I wanted to discuss.

She and David had eaten lunch together the day of the murder, and I needed to find out if David had left her at any time to go backstage. If only I'd been paying more attention that day and not caught up with those darn rewrites, I might have actually seen for myself who'd headed backstage.

The Westwood restaurant turned out to be a nosebleed-expensive joint with exposed brick walls and smooth jazz playing in the background. A few diners sat at linen-clad tables, chatting quietly, the kind of blissfully wealthy people who didn't mind paying full price during happy hour.

Delia was sitting at the bar when I showed up, sipping a martini, looking regal as ever in a black flowy outfit, her raven hair streaked with silver and styled to perfection.

As I slid onto the stool next to her, I noticed she'd ordered a crab cake appetizer.

"Looks yummy," I said, eyeing it hungrily.

"It's fabulous," Delia said. "You should get one, too."

It sure did look delicious—crisp and crunchy on the outside, cooked to golden perfection—and I was more than a tad peckish. I'd been busy that afternoon, coming up with a new slogan for one of my regular clients, Fiedler on the Roof Roofers. (My leading contenders: *We've got you covered! We've got it nailed!* And *We're on top of it!*)

Aside from a few eensy Oreos, I hadn't eaten a thing since lunch.

I was all set to order a crab cake for myself when I saw the price on the menu: $18. No way was I forking over $18 for a single crab cake.

"On second thought," I said, "I'm not that hungry."

Our wannabe actor/waiter approached just then.

"What can I get you?" he asked me, beaming a high-wattage smile just in case one of us was in a position to cast him in a movie.

"House chardonnay."

"Something to eat?"

Not without a bank loan, I refrained from saying.

"No, I'm fine."

"So what did you want to talk about?" Delia asked when he'd gone, spearing a hunk of crab cake. You'd think at the very least she'd offer me a bite. But nada. She just put it in her mouth and started chewing.

"Jaine?" she asked when she'd swallowed. "You asked to meet with me because . . . ?"

Drat. I'd been so focused on that crab cake I almost forgot why I came. Right. The murder.

"As you may have heard, the police seem to be focusing on Aidan as their prime suspect in Misty's murder."

"How absurd! Aidan's far too sweet to be a killer."

"When we were waiting for Detective Jamison to show up after the murder, you said you thought the killer might be David. And I agree. He was furious with Misty."

"I know." Delia chuckled at the memory. "I loved every minute of it."

"You and David had lunch together that day. Did he happen to go backstage at any time?"

"As a matter of fact, he did. Said he was going to the restroom. But, for all I know, he was in the kitchen poisoning Misty's smoothie."

My sentiments exactly.

Our waiter showed up just then with my chardonnay and a big bowl of nuts.

"Here you go," he said. "One house chardonnay and some freshly roasted nuts."

My rescuing angel! I was ready to nominate the guy for Wannabe Actor of the Year.

The nuts were glistening with oil and sprinkled with salt, just the way I liked them. I was just about to reach for a cashew when Delia shoved the bowl aside, shrieking: "*No nuts! Take them away! This instant!!*"

The waiter, cowed, quickly snatched the bowl and hurried off, while well-heeled diners looked up from their meals to give us the once-over. And I couldn't blame them. That had been one heck of an explosion.

"Sorry about that," Delia said with an apologetic shrug. "I can't bear to even look at nuts. Not since my sister died. She was highly allergic to peanuts and went into anaphylactic shock after eating some sea bass prepared with peanut oil at a restaurant. She'd asked if there were any peanut products in the dish and was assured by the restaurant that there weren't.

"They were wrong, and now she's dead. Every time I even think about nuts, I get angry all over again and want to strangle the idiot server who brought my sister that cursed sea bass."

"How awful," I commiserated. "I'm so sorry for your loss."

"Thanks. I've learned to live with it."

After the outburst I'd just witnessed, it seemed she had a lot more learning to do.

"So," I said, eager to get her mind off her sister, "how's everything going with the play?"

"Great, ever since Katie came on board. The play still stinks, of course, but now we're having fun with it. With Misty in the lead, I was afraid the press would be so bad, I'd never work again. Now I think we've got a shot."

She began yakking about *I Married a Zombie*, how it could be a camp classic, maybe even make it to Broadway.

I was barely listening, however, unable to stop thinking about her outburst over the nuts. (And the fact that she *still* hadn't offered me a bite of her crab cake. A single chunk remained on the plate, a chunk she seemed to have forgotten. It was all I could do not to reach over and pop it in my mouth.)

But I digress. Back to Delia and her explosive temper.

I thought about how much Delia hated Misty, how she'd called her Craptessa, and how they'd clashed during rehearsals. Delia just said she'd been afraid the play might put an end to her acting days. Had she seen her reputation irreparably tarnished in what was sure to be—thanks to Misty's godawful performance—a fiasco of a play? Had she bumped off Misty in a moment of madness, desperate to save her career?

Now I wondered what Delia herself had been doing while David excused himself to use the bathroom. Maybe it was Delia, and not David, who'd dashed into the kitchen to tinker with Misty's smoothie.

I'm no criminologist, but in my humble op, I'd say anyone who doesn't offer to share her crab cake is certainly capable of murder.

Chapter Fifteen

Delia may have just leaped onto my suspect list, but my front runner was still David. It was time to pay him a visit, but I needed a pretext for showing up at his doorstep. No way could I let him find out I suspected him of murder.

So I put in a call to him, armed with an excuse I'd just thought up.

"Hi, David," I said when he answered. "It's Jaine Austen. I was hoping I could stop by your apartment tonight. I have a gift for you."

"A gift?"

"A small token of my appreciation for giving me the chance to work on the play."

"That's very nice of you, Jaine, but I'm not really in the mood for visitors. Can you drop it off at the theater?"

"I won't stay long, I promise."

A promise that, of course, I intended to break.

He hesitated a beat before finally saying, "Okay, I guess. Eight o'clock?"

"Great!"

Now all I had to do was get him a gift.

Then inspiration struck. I grabbed my cell phone and headed up the street to the house where my former neighbor, the original Cryptessa, once lived. It was a hellhole when she lived there, but the new owners had fixed it up, so I was able to get a good picture. Which I then printed out.

A quick trip to the drugstore for a frame and gift bag, and voila! I had the perfect present for an *I Married a Zombie* geek.

After a healthy dinner from Sprout's (okay, KFC), I tooled over to David's apartment in Hollywood, an uninspired box of a building pockmarked with protruding room air conditioners.

In spite of a sign out front threatening high-tech security, I was able to breeze through the front door to a closet-sized lobby, where I took the elevator to David's apartment.

David came to the door in shorts and a faded tee, gaunt and hollow-eyed, his hair in Albert Einstein mode. A pair of extraordinarily knobby knees poked out from under his shorts.

"Hey, Jaine," he said, forcing a smile. "Thanks for the gift."

He reached out to take the tote from my hand.

Yikes, was he going to just take it without inviting me in?

I couldn't let that happen.

"Oh, wow!" I said, slithering past him into his living room. "What a neat apartment."

A total lie. The place was a decorating dump, a nerd cave cluttered with nubby brown plaid furniture, a battered wooden coffee table, and a TV hooked up to a veritable tower of ancient VCR and DVD players. Whatever money he'd won from the lottery sure hadn't gone into redecorating.

But I zeroed in on the one feature of the room that stood out.

"I love your photos!"

And indeed, much of David's living room wall was plastered with *I Married a Zombie* posters, as well as autographed photos of the original cast, including a young, redheaded Corky MacLaine as the original Brad Abercrombie.

What a stroke of luck! My "Cryptessa House" pic would be the perfect addition to David's shrine to *I Married a Zombie.*

"For you," I said, finally relinquishing the tote to David.

"Thanks," he replied, tossing it on a small dinette table littered with takeout menus.

"Aren't you going to see what's inside?"

"Okay, sure."

With zero enthusiasm, he reached into the bag and pulled out the picture.

"It's a photo of the original Cryptessa's house. She lived up the street from me."

"Very nice," he said, barely looking at it.

"It should fit right in with your collection."

"Actually," he said, gesturing to his zombie memorabilia, "I'm thinking of taking it all down."

"Really?"

"I'm not into the show as much as I used to be," he said, sinking down onto his sofa. Then he added with a sigh, "Be careful what you wish for, Jaine. When I won the lottery, it was a dream come true. I had the money to bring my favorite sitcom back to life. I got my dream, but it blew up in my face."

"I hear you," I said, parking my fanny on a brown plaid armchair, grateful I hadn't been evicted from the premises.

"I own every episode of the original show, all nine of

them. Whenever I was unhappy or depressed, they always managed to cheer me up. Not anymore."

He stared numbly at the TV across the room, tuned to a decorating show with the sound muted.

"Now I watch *Love It or List It*. Nine times out of ten the people love it. So there's not really any suspense. But at least nobody's a zombie."

His morose musings were interrupted just then by a piercing shriek. Good heavens. Was one of his neighbors being attacked? I was reaching for my cell to call 911 when I realized it wasn't a human shriek, but the shrill whistle of a teakettle.

"That's my tea," David said, making no effort to get up. "I forgot all about it."

"Let me get it for you." I jumped up and headed to a tiny alcove off the living room that served as David's kitchen.

The trash can, I couldn't help noticing, was piled high with empty ramen cups. How sad. Had the guy never heard of Domino's?

"Where are your mugs?" I called out as I turned off the flame under the wailing teakettle.

"In the cabinet to your left."

I opened the cabinet door and saw a bunch of mugs with a picture of the original Cryptessa on them.

"Gee," I said, "I never knew you could buy Cryptessa mugs."

"You can't. I had them specially made up."

Talk about extreme fandom.

"But I don't want a Cryptessa mug now. Bring me one of the others."

It was a choice between Star Trek and Math Geek.

I went with Math Geek.

"Tea's in the cupboard to your right," David called out. "Make yourself a cup if you want one."

"No, I'm good."

I fixed David his tea and brought it out to him.

"Sugar or lemon?" I asked.

"Nah. This is fine." He took the hot mug and put it down on his coffee table without a coaster. My mom would have had a fit. But it didn't really matter. The table was already scarred with a cluster of mug rings.

"What did I tell you?" he said, staring at the silent TV, where a happy couple were grinning in their newly redecorated home. "They love it. They always do."

Okay, time for a much-needed change of subject.

"I'm so sorry about how things went down with Misty," I said. "She wasn't exactly beloved by the other actors, but her death is a tragedy nonetheless."

"I know," he said, gulping back what I suspected were tears.

"Do you have any idea who may have killed her?" I asked.

"I'm pretty sure the cops think it was me."

"You?" I tried to act surprised.

"I guess somebody must've told them how angry I was with Misty the day of the murder."

"Really?" I said, hoping he wouldn't guess that person was *moi*.

"I was furious when I saw her flirting with Aidan. But I didn't kill her. I didn't even have the nerve to confront her. Just wound up sniping at her."

He looked down at his tea, but made no move to drink it.

"I'm so disgusted with myself for falling for Misty in the first place, for being stupid enough to believe she actually cared for me. And I was so damn full of myself during rehearsals. I really was an obnoxious jerk, wasn't I?"

"Of course not," I lied.

"What bothers me most was how badly I treated Becca. Becca, who's sweet and kind and actually loves me. She's worth twenty of Misty. Thank God, she hasn't dumped me. I wouldn't blame her if she did."

With that, tears started trickling out from under his glasses. Tears which quickly turned to sobs.

Oh, dear. I was expecting to confront a killer, not a sobbing math geek.

"Please don't cry."

But the waterworks kept coming.

"Have a Kit Kat bar," I said, fishing one from my purse. "Chocolate is nature's antidepressant, you know. According to my mom, anyway."

David shook his head, now buried in his hands.

"If you don't mind," he said, his voice clogged with tears, "I'd rather be alone."

"Of course."

I got up and took one last look at him sitting on his sofa with his wiry hair and knobby knees, then let myself out of his apartment.

I should have been relieved that the police suspected David. It shifted the spotlight away from Aidan. And me.

And yet I wasn't. On the contrary, I couldn't help feeling sorry for the guy.

I was beginning to think David might not be Misty's killer after all.

Of course, his sorrow just now could have been bogus. He could have been faking his misery with crocodile tears.

But I doubted it. As his performance in the role of Brad Abercrombie had proven, he wasn't that good an actor.

Chapter Sixteen

My investigation was sidelined the next day when I got a phone call from Susie Pearson at the Pasadena Historical Society.

"Good news, Jaine!"

My heart zinged. Was she about to offer me the PR writer's job?

Not quite.

"We've narrowed down our search to two finalists, and you're one of them. We're asking you both to write a sample newsletter to help us make our decision. Is that something you'd be willing to do?"

Not really. No writer ever likes to write freebies. But I couldn't afford to say no.

"Of course!" I chirped. "I'd be happy to."

"Great. I'll send you a list of upcoming events, along with some of our past newsletters so you can get an idea of what we're looking for. I need about a thousand words. Keep it bright and breezy."

And so I spent the next several hours pounding out a sample newsletter, trying my best to sound bright and breezy.

I was in the middle of touting a walking tour of Craftsman homes when the phone rang.

"Hello, Ms. Austen," said an unfamiliar voice. "It's Brandon."

"Brandon?"

"Skyler McEnroe's personal assistant. Calling to remind you of your dinner date with Mr. McEnroe tonight at six."

Omigosh. My bachelor auction date. I'd forgotten all about it.

"Right, sure. Six o'clock."

It was already after five. The minute I hung up, I left my Pasadena Craftsman houses in limbo and hurried off to get ready for my night out.

After a quickie shower, I stood in front of my closet, trying to decide what to wear. ·

I had no idea what kind of restaurant Skyler would be taking me to, so I played it safe with my fallback First Date Outfit: skinny jeans, black turtleneck, silver dangly earrings, and my one and only pair of Manolos.

(Interesting to note that I do not have a fallback Second Date Outfit. Speaks volumes about my love life.)

Up until then, I had zero to low hopes for my dinner with Skyler. What on earth would I have in common with a wheeler-dealer entrepreneur? But then I remembered he was also a patron of the arts. For all I knew he could be a tasteful, caring, sensitive wheeler dealer.

And as I recalled, he was handsome in a slick Vegas croupier kind of way.

In spite of myself, I felt a spark of hope igniting. Was it possible we'd actually hit it off?

By the time I finished dressing, I was having vivid fantasies of me and Sky (by now I was calling him Sky) vacationing in a bougainvillea-covered villa in Tuscany.

"So, Pro," I said, twirling around for her inspection. "What do you think?"

She gazed up from where she was sprawled on the sofa.

I think you should skip the date with the rich guy and spend the night scratching me behind my ears.

If that cat had her way, my fingernails would be surgically attached to the back of her neck.

I'd just given myself a final spritz of perfume when Skyler showed up on my doorstep—looking every bit as slickly handsome as I'd remembered him from the bachelor auction—tall and slim, with a classic Roman nose and curly black hair.

Who knew? Maybe for once the dating gods were on my side.

"A pleasure to meet you, Jaine," he said, flashing me his pearly whites.

"Likewise," I replied in a burst of uninspired repartee.

Soon we were heading down my front path where a shiny black limo was parked out front.

I blinked in disbelief. He'd hired a limo for our date? Just like that, my spark of hope ignited into a roaring fire. I'd obviously hit the dating jackpot.

"Right this way," he said, taking me by the elbow and guiding me to the impressive hunk of metal. But instead of opening the passenger door, he led me up front, seating me in the shotgun side of the driver's area. Then he scooted around the limo and settled in behind the wheel.

"Comfy?" he asked, taking a chauffeur's cap from the dashboard and putting it on his head.

Wait, what?

"You're a limo driver?"

"Yep. Taking a bunch of teenage girls to a slumber party."

And indeed, behind a black-tinted partition, I could hear the raucous squeals of teens in major party mode.

"But I thought this was supposed to be a dinner date."

"It will be, as soon as I drop off the girls in Thousand Oaks."

"Thousand Oaks?" Thousand Oaks happens to be a lovely oak-strewn community, but it was out in the valley. Way out. "That's at least a forty-five-minute drive."

"Yep," he grinned. "It'll give us plenty of time to get to know each other."

Up close, I could see a rather disconcerting blackhead on the side of his classic Roman nose.

Without any further ado, he put the limo in gear, and before I knew it, we were tootling off to Thousand Oaks.

"Skyler, I'm confused. It didn't say anywhere in the auction brochure that you were a limo driver."

"I may have a fudged a bit on my application," he winked. "I figured the auction was a great way to meet a woman of substance."

"If by 'woman of substance' you mean rich, you're out of luck. My checking account is rarely off life support."

"You have a checking account? Cool!"

Oh, groan. I was back in Loser Land, where I usually wind up when I'm foolish enough to venture out on a date.

"It said in the brochure that you're an entrepreneur and patron of the arts."

"I may not be a patron of the arts," he said, "but I *am* a patron of Art's Deli, where every sandwich is a work of Art."

I'd heard about that deli. It was supposed to be great. I only wished I were there right then, scarfing down a pastrami on rye.

"And I'm definitely an entrepreneur. I've been rejected seven times on *Shark Tank*!" he boasted. "Right now, I'm working on my line of What's Cooking? Air Fresheners. Instead of flowers, they smell like food. So far, I've got

Bacon, Burgers on the Grill, Chicken Fajitas, Mamma's Pot Roast, and—for pescatarians—Fish-pourri.

Excitement mounting, he launched into infomercial pitch man mode.

"With What's Cooking? Air Fresheners, you always come home to the smell of a home-cooked meal. It's a proven fact that our sense of smell is responsible for ninety-nine percent of what we taste."

I found that "proven fact" highly dubious.

"Say you're tired after a hard day's work and all you've got in the house is cereal. Well, now you can eat your cereal and fool your brain into thinking it's a burger hot off the grill. Neat, huh?"

Somehow I managed to croak out a feeble, "Uh-huh."

"And that's just one of my ideas. I've got my Dog-brella that keeps your dog dry in the rain, and my glow-in-the-dark slippers, so you can always see where you're going.

"What's more," he said, chest swelled with pride, "I'm also a poet."

Notice, dear reader, that not once had this idiot asked me anything about myself.

"Wanna hear some of my poems? I've memorized all of them."

Lord, no! Unless a poem starts with "roses are red, violets are blue," chances are I'll have no idea what it's about.

But without waiting for my go-ahead, Skyler began his poetry recital.

The bad news was he spent the next half hour spouting what I suspected was very bad poetry. The good news was I could hardly hear him, drowned out as he was by the shrieks of the teenage girls in the back of the limo.

Most of their hilarity involved a guy named Jason with great buns and a girl named Brittany with a botched spray tan.

"Give me back my panties!" I heard one of them holler.

"Not until you give me back my bra!"

As their shrieks grew louder with every passing mile, I got the distinct impression someone had sneaked bootleg booze into the limo.

"It sounds like those girls are drinking alcohol," I said, interrupting Skyler's poetry recital.

"They probably are."

"Aren't you concerned? They're underage. What if you get stopped by the police? You could have your license revoked."

"No problem," he shrugged. "I can always buy another one."

Gaaak! I was riding on the freeway with an unlicensed limo driver!

I white-knuckled it till we finally got to Thousand Oaks, where a bunch of tipsy teenage girls came tumbling out of the limo, chugging cans of alcopop, off to their pajama party.

If only I were going with them. Instead, I was stuck with Skyler McEnroe, unlicensed limo driver.

Whose real name, as I was to discover during dinner, turned out to be Morty (or Marty) Fromkin (or Tompkin). I forget which; I've worked long and hard to repress the memory.

For the purposes of our little saga, let's just stick with Skyler.

Needless to say, there was no "Brandon." The guy who called me to set up the date was Skyler, pretending to be his own personal assistant.

"So we're heading back to town, right?" I asked, once the girls had disappeared into a hulking McMansion.

"Nope. I gotta pick up a couple in Encino and take

them to a restaurant in Beverly Hills. C'mon, help me clean up the mess in back."

Great. Not only was I his terrified passenger, I was now his indentured servant.

And what a mess the back of the limo turned out to be. Candy wrappers and empty alcopop cans were strewn everywhere, along with a lace bra and a stray bunny slipper.

We dumped the trash in a garbage bag and stowed it in the trunk of the limo, along with the bra and slipper.

"You wouldn't believe the stuff people leave behind," Skyler said. "One time I found a leopard-print thong. But it fit okay, so I kept it."

Ugh! Gross! And to think I took a shower for this guy!

"We've got an hour before we're due in Encino," Skyler said, "so let me treat you to dinner."

At last. Something to look forward to. I foolishly hoped for a nice restaurant, but he pulled into the nearest Jack in the Box. Which was actually okay with me. It wasn't Mickey D's, but I like their Jumbo Jacks.

"I'll have a Jumbo Jack with fries."

But that's not what Skyler ordered when he drove up to the clown:

"We'll have two southwest chicken salads."

What the what?

"But I wanted a Jumbo Jack."

"No, we've gotta have salads, so I can show you my latest invention."

With that, he reached into the glove compartment and took out two strange-looking contraptions.

"I call it the 'pfork.' It's a pen on one end and a fork on the other. For people who eat lunch at their desk and want to work while they're eating."

He handed me my pfork, and it was all I could do not to stab him with the tines.

A bored Jack in the Box server gave us our salads, probably the first salads the kid had ever seen on the job.

Meanwhile, Skyler was in seventh heaven, eager to show me his pfork in action.

"Check this out," he said, hanging a clip-on pad from his rearview mirror. "We can play tic-tac-toe while we eat!"

And so I spent what felt like the next several centuries but was probably only a half hour eating a salad I didn't want and playing a game I hadn't played since I was seven years old—all the while trying not to look at the blackhead on Skyler's nose.

When we were finished eating and the pforks were stowed safely back in the limo's glove compartment, we headed off to pick up the couple in Encino—Skyler reciting poems (as I suspected, they stank to high heaven) and chatting about his Dog-brella.

Remember, gang, I'd been with the guy for more than two hours, and he still hadn't asked me a single thing about myself.

We finally arrived at our destination in Encino, where we picked up Skyler's clients, a handsome guy—no doubt an actual entrepreneur and patron of the arts—and his trophy wife. Skyler ushered them into the limo with great fanfare.

"Who's that in the front seat?" the trophy wife asked.

"My trainee," Skyler replied. "As the company's number-one limo driver, I'm showing her the ropes."

My God, the lies flowed from his lips like syrup on flapjacks.

Much to my relief, Skyler didn't recite any more of his poems on the way to Beverly Hills. He'd already run through his repertoire, and besides, he had to stay quiet with the upscale couple in the back of the limo.

I spent much of that quiet time grinding my teeth at the

thought of having forked over $600 for this date from hell.

At last, we pulled up in front of a fancy Beverly Hills restaurant, where the couple disembarked. I watched, envious, as they headed into the restaurant, safely out of Skyler's orbit.

When he sprang back into the limo, he asked if I wanted to stop off at his place for a nightcap.

"No!" I managed not to scream. "Just take me home."

You'd think he would have sensed I sorta loathed him. But not Skyler.

"So, sweetheart," he said as we pulled up to my duplex. "Up for another date sometime?"

Not without general anesthesia.

I mumbled some excuse about chronically bleeding gums, leaping out of the limo before it even came to a complete stop. Then I hurried up the path to my apartment and hid behind my neighbor's azalea bush until I saw him drive off.

Once I was certain he was gone, I got in my Corolla and drove over to the nearest Jack in the Box, where I scarfed down a Jumbo Jack and fries, savoring every bite, grateful it didn't smell like Fish-pourri.

You've Got Mail

To: Jausten
From: Shoptillyoudrop
Subject: What a Fuss!

What a fuss Daddy is making over that darn iguana!

Iggy's still missing, and Daddy's been driving everybody crazy, riding around in his golf cart, calling out "Here, Iggy!" on a bullhorn. The phone has been ringing off the hook with neighbors complaining about the noise.

When he's not aggravating the neighbors, he's moping around the house with Iggy's tiny top hat, moaning, "Don't worry, little fella. I won't give up until I find you."

Not only that, he's posted "Lost Iguana" signs everywhere, offering a $500 reward for the return of his "beloved buddy." $500! This from a man who'll drive clear across town to save 25 cents a pound on honeydew melons.

Time to hit the fudge—

XOXO,
Mom

To: Jausten
From: DaddyO
Subject: Discouraging News

Discouraging news, Lambchop. Still no sign of Iggy, but I haven't given up hope. I won't rest until that little fella is back on my head wearing his top hat.

Gotta run. Someone's at the front door.

Love 'n kisses,
Daddy

To: Jausten
From: DaddyO
Subject: The Nerve of That Woman!

Fasten your seat belt. You won't believe what just happened. That was Lydia Pinkus at the door with a "cease and desist" order for me to stop using my bullhorn in my heroic efforts to find Iggy. She claimed I was in violation of some stupid homeowners association "noise pollution" code.

The nerve of that woman! Not only did she toss Iggy into the wild, now she's trying to stop me from finding him. Clearly, she'll stop at nothing to ruin my chances of bringing home the trophy from the talent show.

But I refuse to be intimidated by her scare tactics. The Battle Axe can threaten me all she wants, but I won't rest until I find Iggy!

Love 'n hugs
From your furious
Daddy

PS. After serving me with that outrageous "cease and desist" order, the Battle Axe had the audacity to invite Mom and me to one of her boring potluck dinners, where she's sure to whip out the same hard-as-a-rock Swedish meatballs she serves at all her dinners. They're like golf balls in cream sauce.

To: Jausten
From: Shoptillyoudrop

Lydia just stopped by to ask Daddy to stop using his bullhorn. A perfectly reasonable request. But the way he's carrying on, you'd think she'd asked him to stop breathing.

She's having a potluck dinner at her house, and Daddy is refusing to go, swearing to never again darken her doorstep.

Which is fine by me. Frankly, I'm relieved to be going by myself. Now I won't have to watch Daddy glower at Lydia all night, making snide comments about her Swedish meatballs. (Which, by the way, happen to be yummy.)

XOXO
Mom

PS. I'm still convinced Iggy is hiding somewhere in the house. I read online that iguanas can go up to two weeks without eating.

To: Jausten
From: DaddyO
Subject: Change of Plan

I'm going to Lydia's potluck dinner, after all.

It just occurred to me: What if Lydia didn't release Iggy into the wild? What if she kidnapped him the day of the book club lunch and is holding him captive in her town house?

I wouldn't put it past her. The woman is the devil in support hose.

I'm going to show up at her potluck dinner, suffer through her Swedish meatballs, and somehow figure out a way to sneak away from the dinner table to find my missing dance partner.

Let Operation Rescue Iggy begin!

Love 'n snuggles from your intrepid
Daddy

Chapter Seventeen

I woke up the next morning, cringing at the memory of my limo date from hell.

"What a disaster!" I cried to Prozac, who was hard at work clawing my chest.

That's what you get for not staying home and scratching my back all night. Now how about some breakfast?

I shuffled off to the kitchen and tossed some Luscious Lamb Lumps into her bowl, still steaming over Skyler and his bogus bio. I was sorely tempted to file a complaint with the Gwyneth Paltrow School of Organic Cosmetology, but I didn't want to waste one more second of mental energy on the guy.

Instead, I fixed myself a CRB, slathered with butter and strawberry jam, which went a long way toward restoring my sanity.

I then spent a productive morning finishing up the Pasadena Historical Society newsletter. And after foolishly opening my emails to read about Daddy driving Tampa Vistas nuts with his bullhorn, I turned my attention back to Misty's murder.

I remembered what Aidan told me about Preston going backstage during lunch hour the day of the murder, ostensibly to call his agent. But what if he wasn't chatting with his ten percenter? What if he'd been busy stirring rat poison in Misty's smoothie?

At first glance, it seemed unlikely Preston was the killer; he'd only worked with Misty for a short time. And yet I could easily imagine Misty making lifelong enemies in fifteen minutes or less.

It was Saturday, a no-rehearsal day, so I decided to pop by Preston's home unannounced. Pouncing on my suspects unawares gives them less time to put up defenses.

According to the contact list Becca had sent me, Preston lived out in the valley, in the well-heeled community of Sherman Oaks. I found his house on a leafy, tree-lined street—a *Leave It to Beaver* Cape Cod with a white picket fence and shuttered windows.

When I rang the bell, a stunning young thing barely out of her teens answered the door.

"Hi, there!" I said. "Is your dad home?"

"My dad? My dad lives in Philadelphia."

"Sorry, my mistake. I'm looking for Preston Chambers."

"Preston's my husband."

Duh. Of course Preston was married to a woman young enough to be his daughter. This was L.A., birthplace of the age-inappropriate relationship.

"And you are?" she asked with a dazzling smile.

"Jaine Austen. I'm a writer on *I Married a Zombie*. I was hoping to talk to your husband about Misty Baines's murder. A friend of mine is a prime suspect in the case, and I'm trying to help clear his name."

"Is that so?" she asked, her interest piqued. "What are you? A private eye?"

"Part-time, semi-professional."

"Wow! A writer *and* a private eye. You sure must lead an exciting life."

"Not really," I said, thinking of my recent ride to hell and back with Skyler.

"It sounds a lot more exciting than modeling. Those photo shoots can take forever. Even if they do fly me to exotic islands all over the world."

Boo frigging hoo. Poor thing had to sit around tropical isles making thousands of bucks an hour. I hated her.

"Preston is at the gym," she was saying. "He's always at the gym. Not me. I can't stand exercising."

Wait. She couldn't stand exercising? I was beginning to warm up to her.

"Besides, I have a really fast metabolism, so I never gain weight."

Nope. I hated her.

"Did Preston ever talk about Misty?" I asked, steering the conversation back to the murder.

"He complained about her all the time. Said she was impossible to work with, that everyone loathed her. From what he told me, I can't say I'm surprised she was killed."

"I thought Preston might have seen something that would point to the killer."

Who could very well be Preston himself, I tactfully refrained from adding.

"I doubt Preston knows anything, but if you want to talk to him, he's at the Sports Club on Ventura Boulevard. You'll probably find him at the treadmills."

"Okay, great. Thanks so much."

I walked back to my car, deep in thought.

Let's recap, shall we? The silver fox, well into his fifties, was married to a stunning model half his age, while I was stuck dating pfork-wielding limo drivers.

And you wonder why I stock my freezer with Chunky Monkey.

* * *

A gang of white-vested valets hung out in front of the Sports Club, an uber-posh gym where the elite meet to get sweaty.

But no way was I going to spring for a valet, not at $16 an hour. Instead, I drove around for what seemed like miles until I landed a spot about ten blocks away.

Between the money I'd saved on valet parking and the calories I was burning, I was feeling quite virtuous as I started out for the gym.

When I finally showed up, more than a tad breathless, I made my way into the lobby—a sparkling-clean affair with white marble floors and a humungous bouquet of flowers at the receptionist's desk. If I didn't know better, I'd have thought I was checking into the Four Seasons.

My plan was to breeze past the reception desk like I was a member, hoping I wouldn't have to show any ID.

Not about to happen.

"Excuse me, ma'am!" called a buff blonde behind the desk. "How may I help you?"

She could start by not calling me "ma'am."

"Just going to work out," I said with a jaunty wave, still trying to bluff my way through.

But the blonde was having none of it.

"Wonderful!" she said, a stiff smile plastered on her face. "May I see your membership card?"

"Oh, drat! I forgot it."

"Sorry, I can't let you in without one."

"To be perfectly honest, Brandi," I said, eyeing her name tag and trying to forge a connection by using her first name, "I'm not a member."

"Okay, let's get you signed up! It's never too late to make fitness a priority." That said with a none-too-subtle glance at my thighs. "What level membership would you like? Our entry silver level starts at $200 a month."

"I don't want to join, Brandi. I just need to dash inside for a few minutes to talk with a friend of mine. And stop staring at my thighs."

No, I didn't add that last part. But I wanted to.

"I can't let you in," Brandi said, her smile now tight as her gluteus, "if you're not a member."

Clearly, chatting her up with her first name hadn't helped.

"Unless," she said, "you want to buy a guest pass."

And so, twenty bucks poorer, I headed into the gym with my guest pass.

Someone pointed me in the direction of the treadmills, and I made my way to a huge room, jammed with enough exercise equipment to keep a third-world nation buffed to perfection.

I spotted Preston on one of the treadmills, in shorts and a tank top, running with impressive speed. For a guy his age, he was in great shape. Heck, for a guy any age, he was in great shape.

"Hey, Preston," I said, scooting alongside his treadmill.

"Jaine!" He looked up in surprise from his "calories burned" display. "What are you doing here?"

I thought about lying and pretending I was interested in joining the gym, but didn't have the energy. That trek from my car plus haggling with Brandi had taken their toll.

"I stopped by your house, and your wife told me you'd be here."

"Excuse me, ma'am." Another buff blond was at my side. This time it was a guy named Lars, in joggers and a Sports Club polo.

I wished everyone would stop calling me "ma'am."

"You can't stand here between treadmills," Lars said. "It's dangerous."

"I won't be here long," I promised.

'Sorry," he said sternly. "Either get on or get out."

With a sigh, I climbed on the treadmill next to Preston's. Then Lars turned it on.

It's a good thing I had a firm grip on the handlebars, because the conveyor belt beneath my feet was moving fast. Lucy-at-the-candy-factory fast.

"Can't you slow it down?" I asked.

"Sorry, ma'am. This is the slowest it goes. It's the setting we use for patients straight out of rehab."

Aack. How embarrassing. There was nothing for it but to put my fanny in gear and keep moving.

"What's up, Jaine?" Preston asked once Lars had gone.

"I wanted to talk to you about Misty's murder," I gasped, struggling to keep up with the treadmill.

"What about it?" asked Preston, legs pumping like pistons, barely breaking a sweat, every silver hair on his head in place.

"The police think Aidan might have done it."

"That's crazy. Aidan's a good kid."

"I know. I was talking to him the other day, and he happened to mention that he saw you going backstage during lunch hour the day of the murder."

Preston turned to glare at me.

"What are you implying? That I had something to do with Misty's death? For your information, I went backstage to call my agent. I was nowhere near Misty's smoothie."

"I didn't think you were," I lied.

By now, I was gasping for air like a beached flounder.

"I was just wondering if you happened to see anyone else backstage while you were there."

That seemed to calm him down.

"Come to think of it," he said, "I saw Delia coming out of the ladies' room."

Very interesting. So Delia had gone backstage during

lunch hour. Funny she didn't mention it when I had drinks with her the other night.

I was simultaneously thinking about Delia's trip back-stage and wondering if my lungs were about to explode when I happened to glance down at Preston's legs, still churning away like pistons.

And that's when I saw it—a tattoo on his ankle. And not just any tattoo—a tattoo of a snake.

I'd seen that tattoo before. But where?

And then I remembered: It was the same tattoo I'd seen in the X-rated photos on Misty's phone the day of the murder, when David confiscated it and had me take it backstage to her dressing room. I flashed back on the im-ages of Misty romping in bed with a mystery man, whose only identifiable feature had been a tattoo of a snake on his ankle.

"Omigosh!" I panted. "You're the guy from Misty's sex photos!"

Preston was so taken aback, he almost tripped on his treadmill. He righted himself just in time and turned off the machine. Then he reached over and—praise be!—turned off mine.

I stepped down with trembling legs, thrilled to be back on terra firma.

"We need to talk," Preston said, grabbing my elbow and leading me out of the exercise room to a secluded area of the corridor.

I should have been afraid—after all, he might very well be the killer—but I was so happy to be off that torture chamber of a treadmill, I followed him, docile as an out-of-shape lamb.

"Yes, I slept with Misty," Preston confessed. "Corky MacLaine warned me she'd be a nightmare to work with, so I was surprised by how friendly she was when I joined the cast. Too friendly. Before I knew it, I wound up at her apartment in her bed. I knew it was a crazy thing to do, but I couldn't help myself.

"The next day she showed me the pictures she'd taken, with that close-up of my tattoo. She threatened to tell my wife if I didn't pay her ten grand. She had me over a barrel. If my wife knew I'd cheated on her, she'd leave me in a flash. And I couldn't bear the thought of losing her."

Having seen his stunning young wife, I understood why.

"The day of the murder, I'd taken money out of the bank to get Misty off my back. But I never wound up paying her. She was killed that afternoon."

"How convenient for you," I pointed out.

"I didn't kill her, though. I swear!"

He seemed to be telling the truth.

But unlike David, Preston was a good actor. For all I knew, he was lying through his perfectly capped teeth.

Chapter Eighteen

"**I** know who killed Misty!" Lance cried.

He and Aidan had come to my apartment, bearing barbeque chicken pizza, to get a progress report on my investigation.

But before I could even begin to tell them what I'd learned, Lance was off and running, in full-blown detective mode.

"No doubt about it," he said. "It was a mob hit!"

"A mob hit? That's ridiculous!" is what I would have said if my mouth hadn't been filled with barbeque chicken pizza.

Which, BTW, was dee-lish.

"Think about it," he said, getting up from the dining table and pacing, channeling his inner Hercule Poirot, practically twirling an invisible mustache and calling us *mes amis.* "Everything we know about Misty says she was trouble with a capital T. Selfish, amoral, scheming. So it makes total sense that she'd be involved with the Mafia, maybe a gangster's moll, or—more likely—a drug dealer!"

His eyes glowed with the prosecutorial fervor of a district attorney up for re-election.

"Aidan says she was always texting during rehearsals. Probably arranging drug drops. So she's dealing drugs, and given what we know about her, it's only a matter of time before she starts skimming money off the top. She thinks she can get away with it, but, of course, she can't. The Mafia kingpins find out, and bam! She's history.

"Voila!" he beamed. "Case solved!"

He stood there, chest puffed with pride, waiting for us to shower him with praise and possibly a ticker-tape parade.

When Aidan and I failed to burst into applause, he looked seriously peeved.

"I agree that Misty was a selfish, scheming brat," I said, "with the ethics of an alley cat."

Prozac looked up from the hunk of barbeque chicken Aidan had tossed her from his pizza.

Hey, watch it. I come from a long line of alley cats.

"But I seriously doubt Misty was a drug dealer," I went on. "Besides, the Mafia doesn't kill people with poisoned smoothies. It's not their MO. If it was a mob hit, Misty'd be at the bottom of the Pacific with a cement block chained to her foot."

"I think Jaine may be right," Aidan said. "This Mafia thing sounds a bit far-fetched."

"Not to me it doesn't," Lance huffed. "What do you think, Pro?" he asked, bending down to sweep her up in his arms.

She wriggled free with an indignant meow.

Lemme go! I was in the middle of a very important piece of chicken!

"Okay, then," Lance said, returning to the dining table and plopping back down in his chair. "If it's not the Mafia, who killed Misty?"

"I don't know," I admitted.

"Hah!" Lance smirked.

"But here's what I've found out so far."

Reluctantly abandoning my pizza, I told them about Misty's affair with Preston and her attempt to blackmail him. And how Delia had been seen going backstage during lunch the day of the murder.

"What about David?" Aidan asked. "Do you think he could have done it? He was furious when he caught Misty coming on to me."

"At first, I was certain it was David. But when I talked with him the other night, he seemed seriously depressed. Pathetic, even. I just don't see him as the killer."

"In other words," Lance said, "you've got nothing."

He needn't look so smug about it.

"Not really," Aidan said, coming to my defense. "If Misty was blackmailing Preston, that's a strong motive for him to have killed her."

"I guess it's possible," Lance conceded, no doubt trying to stay on Aidan's good side. "But I still say it's a mob hit."

"Wait a minute!" Aidan cried, excited. "What about Misty's ex-boyfriend, the one who crashed our morale-boosting dinner? He sure looked like he wanted to kill her."

I'd forgotten about Misty's ex and his angry outburst at the restaurant, reaming into Misty for dumping him for David. And he'd known all about her three o'clock smoothies. Was it possible he'd somehow managed to sneak into the theater to poison his former flame?

"Misty told me they worked together at a restaurant called Mirabella in Santa Monica," Aidan was saying. "I think she said his name was Nick."

"I'll definitely have to check him out!"

"Thanks for all your help, Jaine," Aidan said. "I really appreciate it."

"Yeah, thanks," Lance echoed lamely, still pouting be-cause we hadn't been bowled over by his stupid mob-hit theory.

"Okay," I said, "who wants ice cream?"

"Ice cream?" Major eye roll from Lance. "Honestly, Jaine, sometimes I think you mainline Chunky Monkey."

"Chunky Monkey?" Aidan cried. "I love Chunky Monkey."

Omigosh! A fellow Chunky Monkeyian!

"Actually, I do, too!" Lance said, the little weasel, desperate to score points with Aidan. "I've always admired Jaine's taste in ice cream."

"I love the way the banana chunks meld with the chocolate chunks!" Aidan said to me. "Have you ever tried it with Oreos?"

"All the time!"

I'd found my ice cream soul mate.

"Want some now?" I asked, happy I'd picked some up on my latest trip to the market.

"I'd love some," he said, treating me to a smile almost as yummy as Chunky Monkey.

"Me too!" Lance said, horning in on the ice cream bandwagon.

Prozac, nestled in Aidan's lap, looked up eagerly.

Me too!

We spent the rest of the night watching *House Hunters* and eating Chunky Monkey every time someone said "stainless steel" or "granite."

Aidan also came up with a nifty game of guessing how soon the couple looking for a house would get divorced.

Gosh, he was fun.

By the end of the night, it seemed like everybody at Casa Austen had a crush on the guy.

Chapter Nineteen

Following up on Aidan's suggestion, I decided to pay a visit to Nick, Misty's ex-boyfriend.

I googled the restaurant where he worked and learned that it was open for dinner only, starting at five PM. Which meant Nick had plenty of time to pop over to the theater the afternoon of the murder.

I showed up a little after five, hoping he'd be working that night and that I'd get a chance to talk to him.

I lucked out on both counts.

The restaurant was a stylish joint with a massive mahogany bar, high ceilings, and sparkling white linens on the tables. It was empty when I walked in, except for two elderly ladies enjoying an early-bird dinner.

I spotted Nick right away. The Steve McQueen lookalike who'd lit into Misty with such fervor was tending bar, premium spirits lined up on the shelves behind him, wineglasses hanging from overhead racks. With his close-cropped, sandy hair and ocean-blue eyes, he had the camera-ready good looks of your typical L.A. wactor (waiter/actor).

As I hoisted myself up on one of the stools, he approached me with a tip-inducing smile.

"Hi there, Nick!" I said. "How's it going?"

"Do I know you?" He blinked, puzzled.

"We haven't been formally introduced, but I was in the audience at one of your performances."

"Really?" he asked, thrilled that someone had actually seen him act. "Where?"

"At Trattoria Italiana, the night you came busting in to ream out Misty. You did a terrific job emoting your rage."

His tip-inducing smile vanished.

"I assume you know Misty's been murdered."

"I heard," he said with a curt nod.

"I worked with Misty on the play, and all of us involved in the production are under a cloud of suspicion right now. So I'm asking around, trying to figure out who the killer might be. Not that I think you had anything to do with it," I lied. "I was just hoping you might give me some leads."

"Sorry," he said, decanting some maraschino cherries into a fruit tray behind the bar. "I don't get paid to chat with people who wander in to question me. Especially if those people aren't ordering anything."

I got the hint.

"But I am ordering something. Your house chardonnay."

"You got it."

Seconds later, he was back with a glass of chardonnay.

"That'll be $12."

$12 for a house chard? What a rip-off!

Somehow I managed to tamp down my annoyance and forced a smile.

"Like I was saying, I thought maybe we could chat."

"I don't chat with people who order a single glass of house chardonnay."

Geez, what a grouch.

"How about if I leave your tip in advance?"

As much as it pained me to part with it, I slid a $20 bill across the bar.

That seemed to do the trick.

"So," he said, pocketing it, suddenly Mr. Genial. "How can I help you?"

"Do you know anyone here at the restaurant who might have wanted to kill Misty?"

"Better question," he said with a bitter laugh. "Do I know anybody here who *didn't* want to kill her?

"Nobody liked her. Nobody trusted her. She was notorious for stealing tips. Heck, I was dating her, and *I* didn't trust her. I even installed an app to track her cell phone. That's how I knew she was at Trattoria Italiana that night when I came barging in."

Very interesting. If Nick had been tracking Misty's cell phone, he knew the location of the theater, quite helpful if he'd decided to sneak inside and poison his ex.

Needless to say, I kept this observation to myself.

"Was there anyone in particular who would've liked to see Misty dead?"

"Like I said, everyone hated her. But the one who hated her most of all was our chef, Marc. She ruined his career."

"How did she manage that?"

"One of his customers died from a dish he'd prepared with peanut oil. The customer was allergic to peanuts and went into anaphylactic shock. Misty was the waitress at the table, and Marc warned her about the peanut oil. After the customer died, though, Misty swore Marc never said a word. She got off with a slap on the wrist, and Marc got fired. Word spread, and he was an untouchable in the restaurant community. He finally had to leave the country to get work. But he couldn't have killed Misty. He lives in Abu Dhabi now."

"Omigosh!" I gasped.

"Yeah," Nick said, "it was a shame watching Marc's career go down the tubes."

But I wasn't thinking about Marc or his career. I was thinking about my meeting with Delia at that bar in Westwood, how she'd shrieked at the bartender to take away the bowl of nuts he'd brought over.

I remembered the story she'd told me about her sister dying from an allergic reaction to peanut oil at a restaurant, and Delia's rage at the memory of the dingbat server who'd brought her the fatal dish.

It wasn't tough to connect the dots on this one:

That dingbat server had to have been Misty.

Suddenly, I flashed back on the day of the first table reading, when Delia sat gaping at Misty. At the time, I thought she was reacting to Misty's godawful reading. But what if she'd recognized Misty as the waitress who had, in effect, killed her sister?

Had Delia poisoned Misty to avenge her sister's death? It seemed like a distinct possibility to me.

I was so gobsmacked by this info, I actually stopped eating the side of onion rings I'd ordered when you weren't paying attention.

"I learned my lesson with Misty," Nick was saying. "No more shallow, self-centered actresses for me. From now on, I date only models. And producers. You're not a producer, are you?" he asked, a flirtatious gleam in his Steve McQ baby blues.

"No, just a writer."

"Good enough." He reached under the bar and handed

me an 8x10 glossy photo with his acting credits printed on the back. "Here's my headshot."

I took his headshot and gave him my card, in case he thought of any other bombshell newsflashes he cared to share.

Then, after polishing off my onion rings, I headed outside, armed with Nick's headshot—and the growing conviction that Delia was the killer.

Chapter Twenty

Topping my To Do list the next day was a chat with Delia.

I figured I'd stop by the theater and catch her during lunch. In the meanwhile, however, Prozac was pestering me for a walk, yowling full throttle and practically strapping herself into her harness.

By now, she'd really taken to the great outdoors, a regular Ansel Adams with hair balls.

I put on her harness and leash, and soon we were strolling along my street, Prozac happily sniffing the grass for mummified dog poops and hissing at any squirrel who had the temerity to cross her path.

Halfway up the street, a sprinkler system was on the fritz. Water gushed from one of the sprinkler heads, forming a small river on the sidewalk. Prozac, the same cat who goes ballistic if I come anywhere near her with a wet cloth to wipe mackerel guts from her whiskers, now frolicked in the little stream, splashing around, occasionally pausing to take a few refreshing sips of sprinkler water.

I was a tad distracted, thinking about my upcoming visit with Delia, wondering how to confront her with what I'd learned about her sister's death. So I was totally caught off guard when Prozac abandoned the waterworks and leaped onto a shiny new white Mercedes parked on the street. I gasped in dismay as she tracked muddy paw prints all over the pristine white hood.

"Oh, Pro!" I cried, snatching her in my arms. "Now look what you've done."

She preened with pride.

Neat, huh?

Frantically rummaging in my pocket, I found an old Kleenex and tried to wipe away the paw prints. But all I managed to do was smear them into a big brown blob.

I was just about to race back to my apartment for some water and paper towels when I heard a woman cry, "Oh, no! My new Mercedes. It's filthy!"

Then I heard another, more familiar, voice saying, "I bet the cat did it. That damn cat is a menace to the neighborhood."

I turned to see my neighbor, Mrs. Hurlbutt, the same neighbor whose roast chicken Prozac had attacked so eagerly. Standing next to her was a well-heeled redhead in designer togs, dripping gold jewelry.

"She actually broke into my kitchen and ate my roast chicken," Mrs. Hurlbutt was saying.

"No!" her companion replied, shocked.

In my arms, Prozac gave a petulant meow.

Yeah, and it was sorta dry.

"My cousin just bought this Mercedes yesterday," Mrs. Hurlbutt tut-tutted, "and now it's filthy, thanks to that lunatic little monster of yours."

Prozac bristled.

Hey, who's she calling "little"?

"I'm so sorry," I said. "I was just going home to get some water and paper towels to clean up the mess."

"That won't do," replied the bejeweled redhead. "This car needs to be professionally washed."

"Sure, if you prefer."

"Yes, I prefer. And my car wash charges $20."

Cripes. She expected me to pay for it. First, the guest pass at the Sports Club. Then money to bribe Nick. And now, this. Tracking down Misty's killer was costing me a pretty penny.

Reluctantly, I fished out my wallet and forked over a $20 bill.

"Plus a $5 tip," said the redhead.

"All I've got left," I said, surveying the rapidly dwindling contents of my wallet, "is a ten."

"We'll take it." Mrs. Hurlbutt snatched it from my wallet, making no effort to give me change. "The extra $5 is for pain and suffering."

What nerve! But I couldn't really say anything, not after all the stunts Prozac had pulled on her.

Instead, I apologized once again and started back home.

"Well, young lady, are you proud of yourself?" I asked Pro as I slinked away.

She purred in contentment.

Very.

Wearily, I let myself into my apartment, where Prozac proceeded to track muddy paw prints on my living room floor.

This whole walking-the-cat thing was turning out to be a lot less fun than I thought it'd be.

What a difference a death makes. Without Misty on board, the atmosphere at the theater had gone from a cage match at the Borgias to Happy Hour at TGI Fridays. Gone were the whispered grumblings and snide asides. Now everyone was happy-snappy and pumped about the play.

I showed up toward the end of lunch hour and spotted Delia onstage with Preston. I decided to wait until she was through eating, hoping to catch her alone before rehearsals resumed.

Becca and Katie, the fresh-scrubbed ingenue who'd taken over the role of Cryptessa, were sitting side by side in the audience, heads together, chatting.

Aidan sat a few rows behind them with David, who appeared to be the only one outside the happy bubble, listlessly popping fries into his mouth.

"Hey, Becca," I said, heading over to where she was sitting with Katie.

"Jaine! How nice to see you!" Becca beamed up at me, looking very cute in a T-shirt and overalls, her hair corralled in a pert ponytail.

Was it my imagination, or had she dropped a few pounds?

"I was in the neighborhood, and I thought I'd stop by. How's everything going?"

"Super! Katie is absolutely fantastic as Cryptessa."

"Oh, go on!" Katie said, blushing.

"I mean it," Becca insisted.

"I did, too. Go on. Keep talking me up. I love it!" she said, winking at me.

No doubt about it. The perky blonde was a welcome ray of sunshine here in Zombieland.

"The whole cast has been great," Becca was saying. "Everyone's come up with such terrific suggestions, it's made directing a joy. Of course, David's still in charge," she quickly added. "But he's let me do a bit of directing."

More than a bit, I'd guess. If I weren't mistaken, she was running the show.

"Glad it's all working out so well," I said. "Catch you later."

Then I made my way over to where David was sitting with Aidan.

"Hey, guys. Mind if I join you?"

"Not at all!" Aidan said, patting the seat next to him.

David blushed, probably embarrassed about the tears he'd shed in front of me at his apartment.

"Actually," he said, "I was just going out to take a walk."

With that, he got up and headed for the exit, leaving his bag of fries on his seat.

Can you believe it? Who walks away from a bag of fries? Proof positive the man was seriously depressed.

"You think he's going to finish those?" I asked Aidan when David had gone.

"Nah, help yourself," he said, passing me the fries as I sat down next to him.

"I really shouldn't," I said, grabbing a few.

"Lance and I had a blast at your apartment the other night," Aidan said, polishing off what looked like a yummy turkey and provolone on rye.

"Me too. It's always fun to meet a fellow Chunky Monkey aficionado."

"So how's it going with your investigation?"

"Major breakthrough!"

In a hushed whisper, I told him about my chat with Nick at Mirabella and how Misty was almost certainly responsible for Delia's sister's death.

"No!" he said, when I was through. "So you think Delia killed Misty in revenge?"

"It sure looks like it."

"You know," Aidan said, a pensive look in his eyes, "there's a part of me that wouldn't blame Delia if she'd done it. Misty really was a piece of work."

"Nick said everyone at the restaurant hated her."

"She sure made life miserable around here."

"She probably spent her whole life making people miserable," I said. "I'll bet she was a kindergarten bully, a mean girl in high school, voted Most Likely to Infuriate."

"Absolutely," Aidan agreed.

"I can just picture her torturing the unpopular kids."

But I couldn't sit around trashing Misty. The moment I'd been waiting for had arrived. Delia was getting up and heading backstage.

"Gotta run," I said, jumping up. "I need to catch Delia now, while she's alone."

Grabbing a few fries for good luck, I hurried up the stairs to the stage, racing past Preston, who looked none too happy to see me now that I knew about his sexfest with Misty.

Backstage, I spotted Delia heading for her dressing room.

"Delia, wait up!" I called out.

She turned and saw me.

"Hello, Jaine," she said with a distinctly chilly smile. I wouldn't have been surprised if Preston had been bad-mouthing me.

"Can I talk to you for a few minutes?"

"All right," she said, "but make it short. There's not much time before we start rehearsing again."

I followed her into her dressing room, a cramped box with a beat-up love seat and vanity table. She motioned for me to park my fanny on the love seat, while she sat across from me at her vanity, her spine ramrod straight.

Eyeing her razor-sharp cheekbones and perfectly coiffed hair, I felt like a commoner granted an audience with the queen.

"Okay, I'll get right to the point," I said, plunging in. "I paid a visit to Misty's ex-boyfriend at the restaurant where they worked together. And he told me how Misty served a dish made with peanut oil to a woman who was highly allergic to peanuts. The woman died of anaphylactic shock— just like your sister."

She stared at me, blinking in disbelief, then broke out laughing.

Definitely not the reaction I was expecting.

"What are you saying? That Misty killed my sister? And that I killed Misty to avenge my sister's death?"

"Kinda sorta," I admitted.

"You couldn't be more wrong," she said with a dismissive wave of her hand. "I'll never forget the server who brought my sister that fatal dish, and it wasn't Misty. In fact, the restaurant where my sister died wasn't even in Los Angeles. It was back in Atlanta, where she lived."

I should have been thoroughly embarrassed at that moment. And I would have been, too, if I hadn't googled a newspaper account of her sister's death at Mirabella in Santa Monica, naming the deceased, Pamela Delacroix as the sister of actress Delia Delacroix.

"Atlanta, huh?" I said. "You sure about that?"

I pulled a printout of the news story from my purse and handed it to her.

She read it, and poof. The curtain fell. Her performance was over.

"Okay, you got me," she admitted wearily. "Misty was the incompetent fool who was responsible for my sister's death. That day I first saw her at the table reading, I wanted to lunge across and strangle her. I remembered every inch of her smug little face. But she didn't even come close to remembering me. It was as if she'd killed my sister and blithely gone on with her life without an iota of remorse.

"It was pure torture having to work with her. The day she died I went home and broke open a bottle of champagne. Whoever killed Misty did the world a favor—but it wasn't me."

Was she telling the truth? Or was this just another well-polished act?

"Now if you don't mind, I'd like you to go."

I started for the door when she stopped me.

"Just one more thing, Jaine. You're playing a dangerous game, doing all this snooping. Killers usually play for keeps. You don't want to wind up in the morgue wearing nothing but a toe tag, do you?"

She smiled at me then, an enigmatic smile that left me wondering:

Had I just received some well-meaning advice from an innocent woman?

Or a death threat from a killer?

Chapter Twenty-one

"Check out these espadrilles! Aren't they fabulous?" I was sitting across from Kandi the next day at the Century City mall, eating lunch on their food terrace, an airy space with high-end wooden furniture and planter beds brimming with greenery.

I'd ordered a turkey and provolone sandwich on rye—I'd been lusting after one ever since I saw Aidan scarfing his down at the theater—while Kandi opted for a ceviche appetizer.

I'll never understand people who consider an appetizer a meal. It goes against the laws of nature. But Kandi does it all the time.

She'd just come from a buying spree, choosing a wardrobe for her adventures with Ethan, her yachtsman bachelor. Ethan's boat was still in dry dock, but that hadn't stopped Kandi from investing in a navy blazer, white capris, a red tee with an embroidered anchor on the front, and the above-mentioned espadrilles.

"I just love the way the straps tie around my ankles," she said, holding them up and admiring them.

"Vergle nerf."

I meant to say "very nice," but I'd just taken the first bite of my turkey and provolone on rye.

The espadrilles were pretty nifty, I had to admit, if you didn't mind staggering around on four-inch wedge heels. My personal preference when it comes to summer footwear are flip-flops from La Maison de Rite Aid.

Oblivious to her ceviche, Kandi was now waxing euphoric about Ethan—his fabulously thick hair, his golden tan, the way he managed to look good in wrinkled linen pants, and how his blue oxford shirts brought out the Tiffany blue in his eyes.

I nodded through it all, only half-listening, thinking about how divine turkey tasted with provolone cheese.

"The other night, we watched a fascinating documentary about a husband and wife who sailed around the world," she said. "Ethan wants us to do that. Doesn't that sound exciting?"

"I'm not so sure. You realize there are no mani-pedis at sea. Or facials. Or champagne brunches. It's a lot of hard work, with very few showers."

"Of course, I know all that," she said with a dismissive wave of her fork. "Before meeting Ethan, I would have agreed with you. But not now. Now I can't wait to set sail on the open seas!"

At last, she remembered she was supposed to be eating and took a bite of her ceviche.

"Omigosh," she said, before she could get to Bite Two. "I've been talking so much about Ethan, I almost forgot to ask. How did your date go with your entrepreneur and patron of the arts?"

"Total fiasco," I said, groaning at the memory.

"Oh, no!" Kandi said, eyes wide with sympathy. "What happened?"

I proceeded to tell her about my date from hell with Skyler, how he'd faked his way into the bachelor auction, hoping to meet a rich woman. How he dragged me out to

Thousand Oaks with a bunch of screaming teens. And how he took me to dinner at Jack in the Box, where I had to eat my salad with his stupid pfork, all the while boring me senseless with his bad poetry.

"You had a salad?" Kandi nodded in approval. "Good for you!"

I blinked at her in disbelief.

"That's your takeaway from this nightmare? That I ate a salad?"

"No, I agree the date sounds pretty bad. I'm going to contact the Gwyneth Paltrow School of Organic Cosmetology and see if I can get you your money back."

"Would you? That'd be great."

"Not a problem. So when are you seeing him again?"

"Wait. What part of 'I hated this guy' don't you understand? Why on earth would I see him after that awful date? And by the way, I neglected to mention that in the entire three and a half excruciating hours we spent together, he never shut up, never once asked me a single question about myself."

"Some guys do that incessant chatter thing when they're nervous. He might be a lot better on a second date."

"I'm sure as heck not going to be around to find out."

"Let's not be so hasty, honey," she said, taking my hands in hers, which I found more than a bit annoying since she was cutting off access to my sandwich.

Looked like I was about to get one of Kandi's patented positive-thinking pep talks.

"True, Skyler faked his way into the bachelor auction. But at least he was honest enough to admit he was looking for someone rich to date. And after all, so were you."

"No, I wasn't looking for someone rich! I was looking for my chocolate mousse cake!"

"You need to think of Skyler as dating practice. If you stay home all the time watching HGTV with Prozac, your dating skills will atrophy. And you can't let that happen. It's like a muscle. You've got to use it or lose it. Promise me you'll give him another chance."

"I promise," I lied. Anything to get her to let go of my hands.

The only thing I cared about exercising right then were my taste buds. And after polishing off my turkey and provolone on rye—along with a pickle and a bag of BBQ chips—I'm happy to report they got quite a workout.

You've Got Mail

To: Jausten
From: Shoptillyoudrop
Subject: What a Disaster!

We just got back from Lydia's potluck dinner. What a disaster!

On the drive over, Daddy told me about his crazy plan to sneak off and search for Iggy while the rest of us were eating. As much as I tried, there was simply no talking him out of it. He didn't even balk when I threatened to stop making meatloaf for a month. I should have insisted he turn around and drive back home, but I didn't feel right about canceling on Lydia at the last minute.

Everything was fine at first. We all showed up with our contributions to the dinner. I brought baked ziti and an emergency box of fudge. Edna Lindstrom brought her delicious string bean salad and a chocolate bundt cake for dessert. Bill and Nancy Boyarsky brought scalloped potatoes and dinner rolls. And Nick Roulakis, bless his heart, brought several bottles of wine.

Lydia served drinks in the living room, along with a yummy feta cheese and spinach puff-pastry appetizer.

"I stole the recipe from Ina Garten," she confessed.

"That's not all she stole," Daddy muttered under his breath.

Soon we were seated at the dining room table, chatting and having a wonderful time. Well, everyone else was having a wonderful time. I was too busy worrying about Daddy and his idiotic plan to "rescue" Iggy. Sure enough, the minute Lydia brought out her Swedish meatballs, Daddy excused himself to use the bathroom.

I sat there, cringing at the thought of Daddy sneaking around Lydia's town house. At one point, I heard his footsteps clomping overhead, but thank heavens everyone was chattering away, and no one else seemed to notice.

At last, Daddy came back to the dining room, looking peeved. Clearly he'd failed in his mission to find Iggy, which came as no surprise to me. I can assure you, sweetheart, that the president of the Tampa Vistas Homeowners Association and cultural leader of our community does not go running around stealing iguanas.

The rest of the dinner continued without incident, until Lydia brought out Edna Lindstrom's chocolate bundt cake. She was just about to slice into it when Daddy jumped up from his seat.

"Aha!" he cried. "I knew it! I knew it all along!"

"What on earth are you talking about?" Lydia asked.

"You kidnapped Iggy, my iguana, to keep me from winning first prize at the talent show."

"I did not kidnap your silly iguana!" Lydia said.

"Oh, really? Then why do I see him hiding behind a throw pillow on your living room couch?"

He pointed across to the living room, and, sure enough, I could see some reptilian scales peeking out from behind a throw pillow. For a moment, I was flummoxed. Had Daddy been right about Lydia? Had she actually kidnapped Iggy?

Daddy raced over to the sofa, the rest of us hot on his heels.

"Behold!" he cried. "My beloved Iggy!"

Then he whipped away the throw cushion, only to reveal Edna Lindstrom's pleather snakeskin purse. Which, I must confess, was pretty much the same color as Iggy.

I didn't think I could possibly be more embarrassed, but I was wrong. Because just then Lydia pointed down the hallway and cried, "Is that water seeping out from the bathroom?"

It sure was. Daddy had turned on the faucet in the guest bathroom to make everyone think he was in there while he searched Lydia's town house, but then forgot to turn it off. It had been running all this time.

It took us a good forty-five minutes to clean up the mess.

Lydia will be sending us an estimate to replace the carpet in her hallway.

I'm so mad, I could spit!
XOXO
Mom

To: Jausten
From: DaddyO
Subject: Minor Mishap

Disappointing news, Lambchop. I wasn't able to find Iggy at Lydia's town house. (But I'm sure she's got him hidden there somewhere.)

In the course of looking for him, I left the water running in the guest bathroom, and a tiny bit overflowed from the sink. From the way your mom is carrying on, you'd think I'd just sunk the Titanic. I don't see why she's making such a fuss. We mopped up the water in no time.

And get this. Lydia had the unmitigated gall to bill us for what she's calling "carpet damage." Please! It was a few drops of water; I'm sure it'll dry out in no time.

I must admit I'm very disappointed in Mom. Instead of backing me up in my valiant effort to rescue Iggy, she's in a lather about a minor bathroom mishap.

Love 'n snuggles
from your unjustly maligned,
Daddy

Chapter Twenty-two

Back in my car, I checked my cell phone and found a text from Detective Jamison, summoning the cast and crew of *I Married a Zombie* to the theater at eight p.m. that night.

I wondered if there'd been a break in the case. Or maybe she wanted to question us again. At that moment, Delia was my prime suspect, but who knew what the police had uncovered?

I spent the rest of the afternoon trying to write a speech for Toiletmasters' president, Phil Angelides, to give at the next meeting of the L.A. Plumbers Association. But Prozac wasn't making it easy for me, sitting at the door with her halter, meowing for a walk.

"Forget it, Pro. I can't risk another paw-prints-on-a-Mercedes episode."

Eventually she gave up and amused herself, as I was later to discover, clawing a hole in my quilt.

After a quick dinner of Cheerios and Oreos—getting my minimum daily requirement of vitamin O—I started out for the theater.

For once, L.A.'s normally hellish traffic was light, and I sailed over, showing up at the theater about five minutes early. I headed inside past the lobby into the auditorium and saw I was the first to arrive.

Taking a seat in one of the back rows, I opened my phone to check my emails, only to read about Daddy's mortifying antics at Lydia's potluck dinner.

And still no word from the Pasadena Historical Society. Darn. I was lusting after that prestigious gig and the much-needed dose of refinement it would add to my résumé.

By now, it was a few minutes after eight, and I was the only one in the theater. Something about this didn't feel right. Where was everybody else? And why had Detective Jamison summoned all of us here in the first place? If she wanted to question us, why not do it at police headquarters?

"Hello!" I called out. "Anybody here?"

Dead silence.

I glanced up at the stage, and for the first time, I noticed a prop headstone in the middle of the living room set. How odd. What on earth was it doing there, next to the coffee table? Odder still, it looked like something had been painted on it.

With no small degree of trepidation, I made my way down the aisle and up the steps to the stage to get a better look. As I approached the headstone, a jolt of fear hit me in my gut, sending my Cheerios and Oreos roiling. For there on the papier-mâché prop someone had spray-painted the words RIP JAINE AUSTEN—complete with bright red splotches, undoubtedly meant to be blood.

Then, as if I weren't terrified enough, the lights suddenly went out—leaving me in the pitch dark, unable to see a thing.

Oh, Lordy. There was no police meeting. Someone had faked that text to lure me to the theater. The same someone who'd killed Misty. And now he (or she) was out to kill me!

How on earth was I going to get back down to the seating area in the pitch dark? I couldn't risk trying to find the stairs. What if I took a step in the wrong direction and fell off the stage? If only I had my cell phone, I could have turned on the flashlight. But I'd left it in my purse in the back of the theater.

Unwilling to risk a fall, I got down on my fanny and scooted forward till I reached the edge of the stage.

Then I took a deep breath and jumped.

I had visions of breaking a bone or two, but fortunately it wasn't much of a fall, and the floor was carpeted. So I managed to land without any injuries and sent up a tiny prayer of thanks to Ben and Jerry for the natural padding on my tush.

Scrambling to my feet, I stumbled around, bumping into seats in the front row until I finally reached the aisle. Using the aisle seats to guide me, I lurched toward the exit.

Just when I was beginning to think I was out of harm's way, I heard footsteps behind me. My heart plummeted. But I reminded myself that whoever was chasing me was just as much in the dark as I was.

I forced myself not to panic and continued feeling my way up the aisle until at last I reached the door to the lobby. I pushed it open, my heart beating like a bongo, thrilled to see street light filtering in from under the front door. In a last frantic rush, I dashed outside.

After my heart finally stopped pounding, I decided to call the police and let them know what happened. Maybe they could even catch the killer.

But then I remembered: My phone was in my purse, back in the theater.

No way was I going back in there, not without a police escort.

I looked around for someone whose cell phone I could borrow.

The only person in sight was a tall woman standing at the corner. As I scooted over to her side, I saw she was wearing a bustier and leather skirt so tight, it was practically a tourniquet. A Dolly Parton waterfall of a wig, sky-high platform shoes, and a necklace with the name PEACHES spelled out on her chest completed the look.

From her extraordinarily well-developed muscles and the faint trace of a five o'clock shadow under her makeup, I figured this was either a woman in serious need of hormone treatments or a guy in drag.

"Excuse me . . . . er . . . ma'am?"

Peaches turned and checked me out.

"Sorry, hon. I don't do women."

It looked like I'd met my first drag-queen hooker.

"That's okay," I said, the words tumbling out of my mouth in a nervous babble. "I just need to use your phone. It's an emergency. I left my purse in the theater, but I'm afraid to go back inside in case the killer with the bloody headstone is still there."

Peaches lobbed me a serious eye roll.

"Hey, girl. What uppers are you on? Bennies? If so, got any to share?"

"I'm not on any meds. Please, can I use your phone to call the police?"

"All right," she said, handing it over, "but I hope you realize I'm going to have to change my street corner for you. Can't stay here and be hassled by the cops."

Practically ripping the phone from her hand, I punched in 911. Somehow I managed to give the police the address of the theater and tell them about being trapped there with the killer and the purse I'd left behind in my flight to freedom.

"Thanks so much," I said to Peaches when I was through. "How can I ever repay you?"

"Give me some love, sweetcakes!"

Needless to say, she was not talking to me, but to some guy driving by in a Maserati.

I wished her good luck on her new street corner and headed back to the theater to wait for the police. It felt like hours, but it was probably only minutes before they showed up.

"What exactly happened?" asked a burly cop with muscles almost as ripped as Peaches's. "According to the nine-one-one operator, you were trapped alone in the theater with someone you believe is a killer. Were you able to identify your assailant?"

"No, it was pitch dark in there."

"What makes you think this person is a killer?"

I told them about Misty's murder and how I'd gotten a fake text from Detective Jamison summoning me to the theater.

"When I showed up the theater was empty except for the bloody headstone with my name on it and suddenly the lights went out and I had to slide on my fanny to jump off the stage but when I ran up the aisle I heard footsteps behind me and was too scared to get my purse."

I really had to get a handle on this babbling-when-nervous thing.

"Looks like we've got another nutcase on our hands," Officer Muscles said to his partner, a stocky guy with a Marine buzz cut.

Okay, so what he really said was, "Let's go inside."

But I knew what he was thinking.

He took a flashlight from his holster and turned it on before opening the door.

I blinked in surprise to see that the lights were on.

"I thought you said the lights were off."

"I guess the killer must have turned them back on."

"Is that your purse?" he asked as we entered the auditorium, pointing to the seat where I'd left it.

"Yes," I said hurrying over to retrieve it.

"So where's that bloody headstone you were talking about?" asked his partner, who'd made his way onto the stage.

I looked up and saw the headstone was gone.

"I swear it was there, right next to the coffee table." I hurried up to the stage, Officer Muscles right behind me. "Maybe the killer hid it back in the prop area."

I started backstage, then stopped abruptly.

"Wait! What if the killer's still here, waiting to attack?"

The cops exchanged highly skeptical looks.

"You stay here, ma'am," said the stocky cop. "I'll check it out."

I couldn't help noticing he wasn't even bothering to reach for his gun as he headed toward the prop-storage area. He obviously didn't believe there was a killer lurking on the premises.

"All clear, ma'am," he called out seconds later. "Nobody here."

Officer Muscles and I headed over to join him.

"Is that the tombstone you were looking for?" Officer Muscles asked, pointing to a graffiti-free headstone.

"No, the one I saw said 'RIP Jaine Austen.' It's got to be here somewhere."

Then I remembered the cellar where Misty tried to take Aidan for whoopsie doodle.

"There's a cellar below us," I said, pulling up the trapdoor. "I bet it's down there."

"I'll take a look," Officer Muscles said.

He began his descent to the cellar, and soon I could hear him walking around.

After a while, he came back up.

"Nothing down there but some Playbills and an old mattress."

It looked like the killer had fled, taking the bloody headstone. But how did they get away without me noticing? I was out on the sidewalk the whole time. Maybe they made a run for it while I was talking to Peaches.

The cops were escorting me back to the stage when we passed the rusty side door I'd seen the exterminator using when he showed up with those mousetraps.

"I know where the killer went!" I cried. "Probably slipped out this side door."

"Okay, we'll check outside for the killer," Officer Muscles said.

I could practically see air quotes around the word "killer."

"In the meanwhile, why don't you go home and relax. Sometimes when we're stressed, our minds can play tricks on us."

He *so* had me pegged as a nutcase.

"Would you like us to arrange for someone to drive you home?"

"No, I'm fine."

But I was far from fine.

Back home, I tried to call the number from the phony Jamison text, only to hear a recorded message: *This number is no longer in service.* Whoever sent the text had probably used a burner phone to scare the living daylights out of me.

And it had worked. Big-time.

Chapter Twenty-three

True, my close encounter with a headstone had shaken me to the core. But I woke up the next morning with renewed confidence, determined to continue my investigation.

Just goes to show what a good night's sleep and a restorative dose of Chunky Monkey can do.

I got out of bed with a spring in my step—a spring that didn't last very long, thanks to Prozac darting around my ankles demanding to be fed.

Soon, she had her little pink nose buried in a bowl of Hearty Halibut Innards while I set about nuking a cinnamon raisin bagel.

Just as I was slathering it with strawberry jam, the phone rang.

"Hi, Jaine!" Becca's voice came sailing across the line. "Can you stop by my place this afternoon around four? I've got exciting news!"

"Sure," I said, wondering what was on her agenda, and hoping I wasn't being lured into another trap.

Her place turned out to be a one-room studio behind a bungalow in Santa Monica. I parked my car, then headed up a flagstone path past the bungalow—grateful not to find any bloody headstones en route. I soon found myself in a fairy-tale backyard, lush with a riot of flowers straight out of *Martha Stewart Living*. In the middle of it all was Becca's white clapboard studio, French doors at the entrance flanked on both sides by pink and white hollyhocks. A tiny patio out front boasted an Adirondack chair and a potted hibiscus.

For a computer geek, she sure had great taste in real estate. Apparently, there were many sides to Becca I had not yet discovered.

The French doors were open, and the aroma of something yummy in the oven wafted out to greet me.

"Hey, Becca," I called out. "It's me, Jaine."

Seconds later, Becca came hurrying to the door wearing an apron, her cheeks flushed, swiping her bangs from her forehead.

"C'mon in," she said, ushering me inside.

A bright red sectional sofa and a coffee table took up the front of the unit, with a kitchenette and bistro table off to the side, and a bed and armoire in the rear.

"Whatever you're cooking," I said, breathing in the heady aroma, "smells great."

"It's pot roast. David's favorite. He's coming over later for dinner."

It looked like that relationship was off life support, still alive and kicking.

"Can I get you anything?" Becca asked. "Coffee? Water? Juice?"

"No, I'm good."

What I really wanted was that pot roast.

"Guess what?" Becca said, as we sat across from each other on her sectional. "I'm throwing a 'Come as a Zombie' party!"

Say, what?

"When I went to order the costumes, I found some terrific hooded capes for the zombies. White for Cryptessa, red for Catatonia, and black for Uncle Dedly.

"Let me show you!"

She hurried to her armoire and came back wearing a long red hooded cape.

"Isn't it fantastic?" she asked, swirling around and modeling it.

I looked at the flowing cape with its deep hood. The whole effect was indeed quite dramatic.

"I loved the capes so much," Becca was saying, "I decided to throw a costume party, where all the guests will wear zombie capes. There's a great online site where I can buy plastic capes in bulk. Doesn't that sound fun?"

Not really.

"Yes, fun," I managed to say.

"I'll have it catered, of course. Nothing fancy. Just franks-in-a-blanket. Pizza pockets. Bagel bites. Stuff like that."

She had me at franks-in-a-blanket.

"Sounds great!"

This time I meant it.

"We need to create a buzz for the show before it opens. So we'll be inviting the press and social-media influencers. And that's where you come in, Jaine. I'm hoping you can write up a press release as well as a party invitation."

"Of course," I assured her.

"We'll host it onstage at the theater. I'll text you the time and date and other details."

Just then her oven timer dinged, and she jumped up, tossing the cape on the sofa.

"Time to put my scalloped potatoes in the oven!"

As she scurried over to the tiny kitchenette, I could see the bistro table had been set for two, with candles and a vase of daisies.

I watched Becca bustling around the kitchen, happy snappy, basking in her resurrected relationship with David, not to mention her ever-expanding role as the play's producer/director. What a far cry from the wounded creature she'd been when Misty was on the scene stealing David out from under her.

If anyone had a motive to kill Misty, it was Becca.

But Becca was gone from the theater the day of the murder, running errands and ordering costumes.

Or was she?

I suddenly remembered that rusty side door at the theater—the one used by the exterminator and last night's mystery stalker.

Who's to say Becca hadn't taken a break from her errands and used that side door to sneak back to the theater and poison Misty's smoothie? Who's to say she hadn't used it last night to scare the living kapok out of me?

Last night's stalker had to have a key to the theater. And as one of the show's producers, Becca surely must have had one.

The more I thought about it, the more convinced I became that the woman popping scalloped potatoes in her oven could very well be my mystery stalker and—even more important—Misty's killer.

"David adores scalloped potatoes," she was saying, rejoining me on the sofa.

"So things are good with you two?" I asked.

"Couldn't be better! David's been a perfect angel. He sent me those flowers," she said pointing to the daisies on her bistro table. "I thought I'd lost him for sure when Misty was cast as Cryptessa. He became a totally different person. But he's back to his old self now, the same kind, caring guy I met four years ago at a Comic-Con convention."

She continued to gush about David, but I wasn't really paying attention, my mind filled with images of Becca tiptoeing into the theater's kitchen and making a beeline for the rat poison.

She was in the middle of waxing euphoric about a *Star Trek* sleep shirt David had given her when Katie appeared at the open French doors.

"Oh, hi, Jaine," Katie said, catching sight of me. "I didn't know you were here."

"I was just telling Jaine about our 'Come as a Zombie' party," Becca said. "She's going to write up a press release."

"Doesn't it sound super?" Katie asked.

"Super!" I agreed, remembering those franks-in-a-blanket.

"Here, honey," Katie said to Becca, reaching into her handbag and holding up a pair of sparkly crystal earrings. "I brought you these to wear for your dinner with David tonight."

"I love them!" Becca cried.

She wrapped Katie in a bear hug, and then they both plopped down across from me on the sectional, Becca blathering about how Katie was the best Cryptessa ever, and Katie blathering about how grateful she was to be in the play.

Once again, my mind wandered, this time thinking about those scalloped potatoes bubbling in the oven. I was fantasizing about scooting over to the kitchen and nabbing myself a bite when Becca said something that made me perk up and pay attention.

"I knew Katie was right for the part the minute I saw her audition. We've kept in touch ever since and have become good friends."

"Really good friends!" Katie added with a grin.

Whoa! If Becca and Katie had been in touch ever since the audition, it meant Becca could have easily told Katie about Misty's three-o'clock smoothie routine.

Maybe it wasn't Becca who sneaked into the theater the day of the murder to poison Misty's smoothie. Maybe it was Katie. Had she been willing to literally kill for a part?

Or maybe the two newly minted BFFs were in it together, joining forces to get rid of their mutual enemy.

I left the two of them chattering on the sofa and headed back down the flagstone path to my car.

Driving home, I kept thinking about that key to the theater. Whoever terrorized me last night had to have had one. My money was on Becca, perhaps aided and abetted by her new bestie, Katie. But I had to find out for sure.

The minute I got home I texted Aidan, asking if anyone other than David and Becca had a key to the theater.

We all do, he texted back. **Becca gave the actors keys in case we wanted to use the theater for impromptu rehearsals.**

Oh, drat. There went my airtight case against Becca.

Any one of the actors could have let themselves into the theater last night.

How very irritating.

Luckily, I was able to mellow out with meditation, deep-breathing exercises, and the scalloped potatoes and franks-in-a-blanket I'd picked up at the market on my way home.

Chapter Twenty-four

Becca texted me the party details, and bright and early the next morning, I was at my computer, banging away at the invite and press release. The invite was easy, but I must confess I struggled with the press release, trying to sound peppy about a project I sort of loathed.

I had to slog through several drafts before I finally came up with an enthusiastic version that would pass muster with Becca. For your edification, and to give you an insight into the writer's process, here's the first draft and the final draft of my press release.

"Come as a Zombie" Party Press Release
First Draft
In one of the most disastrous theatrical decisions since Abe Lincoln chose to pop by the Ford's Theater, novice producers David Garber and Becca Washton are bringing the long-forgotten—and for good reason!—sitcom I Married a Zombie *back to life at the Mayfair Theater in Hollywood. Featured in the cast are veteran actors Delia Delacroix and Preston Chambers, along with newcomers Aidan Rae and Katie Gustafson (all of whom are hard at work expunging any mention of*

this train wreck from their résumés). The production has been plagued from the get-go by mice, murder, and petrified bran muffins. In a desperate attempt to drum up ticket sales from people other than their relatives, the fledgling producers are throwing a "Come as a Zombie" party.

Partygoers are encouraged to come dressed as zombies. Theater lovers are encouraged to stay home and watch Netflix.

"Come as a Zombie" Party Press Release
Final Draft

Wonderful news, theater lovers! A hilarious new play based on the beloved sitcom I Married a Zombie *is coming soon to the Mayfair Theater in Hollywood.*

"It's been a long-time dream of mine to bring this comedy classic to the stage," says producer David Garber. "And we're thrilled to have veteran actors Delia Delacroix and Preston Chambers on board," adds co-producer Becca Washton, "along with newcomers Aidan Rae and Katie Gustafson." According to the producers, Ms. Gustafson is "positively radiant" in the part of Cryptessa, the irrepressible zombie with a heart of gold. To celebrate what's sure to be a box office smash, the producers are throwing a "Come as a Zombie" party. The party's theme is "Show up undead, and have the time of your life!"

Refreshments will be served.

I'd just sent off the final draft to Becca when the phone rang, an unfamiliar number showing up on my screen.

Like a fool, I answered it.

"Hi, Jaine. It's me, Skyler."

Oh, lord. The pfork-wielding, poetry-spouting limo driver. Why, oh, why couldn't it have been a telemarketer?

"I was hoping we could see each other again," he said.

I was on the verge of issuing a polite but emphatic "Never in a zillion years!" when something made me stop. I thought of Kandi and how happy she was with Ethan. And how Lance had found a terrific guy like Aidan. My best friends were both in love, and I was still stranded in a singles wasteland.

Maybe Skyler wasn't so bad after all.

I remembered what Kandi said about how men often talk too much when they're nervous. Maybe Skyler had been nervous on our date. Maybe that's why he rattled off his poetry nonstop. Maybe once I got to know him, he'd be a really nice guy.

At the very least, going out with him would, as Kandi said, give me a chance to flex my dating muscles.

Years ago, I'd read some words of wisdom (either from Sophocles or Ask Amy, I forget who). At the time, I brushed them aside, but now they were ringing in my ears, loud and clear:

Say Yes to Everything!

Perhaps it was time for me to stop putting out so much negative energy and start saying "yes" to life.

I've never actually dived off a high diving board, but I imagine it must feel like I felt when I took a deep breath and said to Skyler:

"Okay, sure."

"I know it's last-minute, but are you free for lunch today?"

Usually I'd say no to a guy's last-minute invite, but not today.

"Yes, I'm free."

"Great! I want to take you to a terrific all-you-can-eat buffet."

An all-you-can-eat buffet? Color me there!

"Can you be ready in a half hour?"

"Absolutely!"

"Wear something nice. It's going to be pretty fancy."

Wow, a buffet lunch at a fancy restaurant. I really had to start saying yes to everything more often.

I raced to my bedroom and changed into my one and only Prada pantsuit, accessorized with pearl studs and my trusty Manolos. When I was good to go, I headed back to the living room.

Prozac, who was sprawled out on my computer keyboard, looked up, distinctly annoyed.

Where are you going all dressed up? You can't leave! It's time for my midday belly rub.

There had to be exceptions to this "Say yes to everything" rule, and Prozac's belly rub was definitely one of them.

"Sorry, kiddo. I'm off to a fancy buffet lunch."

Just as I was grabbing my purse—a new Coach tote I'd picked up half-price at Nordstrom—Skyler showed up on my doorstep, immaculately groomed in a tailored black suit, his dark curls slicked back, smelling quite yummy in a spicy aftershave. I hadn't noticed it before, but in the bright light of day, I could see he had lovely hazel eyes.

True, he still had the slightly louche look of a Vegas croupier, but I could live with that.

"I'm so happy you could make it on such short notice," he said. "You look terrific!"

"Thank you," I replied, blushing just a tad. Those hazel eyes of his were really quite appealing.

As we headed down the front path, I prayed he wouldn't be driving a limo with a passel of passengers in back.

Luckily, there was no limo in sight when we got to the curb. (Hurray!) Instead, he led me to a vintage red Miata sports car. After helping me in, he hopped in beside me.

"Before we go," he said, reaching into his glove compartment, "I have a present for you."

For a frightening instant, I thought he was going to pull out a pfork.

But much to my surprise, he handed me a small jewelry box.

Inside was a faux emerald-and-diamond ring, a honker piece of green glass surrounded by tiny white "diamonds." He'd probably picked it up for ten bucks at the 99 Cent Store, but it was actually pretty cute.

"Gee, thanks," I said, slipping it on, hoping my finger wouldn't soon turn as green as the "emerald."

"It's my way of apologizing," he said as we took off in the Miata. "I did so much talking the other night, I never did get to ask you anything about yourself. So tell me," he added, beaming me a warm smile, "all about Jaine Austen."

So Kandi was right about guys yakking too much when they're nervous.

I proceeded to tell Skyler about my life as a freelance writer, working for small clients like Toiletmasters and Tip Top Dry Cleaners, about my latest adventure as a script doctor, and my hopes for landing a job with the Pasadena Historical Society.

"Wow!" he said when I was through. "I can't believe I'm riding in the same car with the woman who wrote *In a Rush to Flush? Call Toiletmasters!* That is so cool."

Then we had an actual conversation. You know, where he said something and then I said something and then he said something. I told him about Prozac, and he told me about his dog, Chester. We talked about our favorite writers (him, John Grisham; me, Anne Tyler), movies, and TV shows. I was happy to learn he wasn't one of those insufferable snobs who brag that they never watch TV. He liked TV almost as much as I did, and we eagerly filled each other in on what we'd been streaming.

So caught up was I in our conversation that I wasn't really paying attention to where we were going.

"Here we are," Skyler said, pulling up in front of a beautiful Tudor home on a hilly suburban street.

I blinked, puzzled. "I don't understand. I thought we were going to a restaurant."

"Oh, no. This is a private gathering," he said, hopping out of the car, and running to open the passenger door for me.

Was he taking me to meet his friends? So soon? It seemed a bit premature. After all, this was only our second date. But what the heck? I was saying Yes to everything.

So I followed him up a flight of stairs to this rather grand house, prepared to mix and mingle with his besties.

The front door was open when we reached the top of the stairs, and we headed inside. I looked around and saw clusters of people, chatting somberly, all dressed in black.

Either these were a bunch of sophisticated New Yorkers or—no, it couldn't be. A horrible thought popped up in my brain, but I batted it away as Skyler ushered me over to a wan brunette seated on a sofa, surrounded by several other people, some of whom had tears in their eyes.

"I'm so sorry for your loss," Skyler said, taking the brunette's hand.

Aack! My worst fears had come true. We were at a funeral reception!

"How did you know Grandfather?" the woman was asking Skyler with a polite smile.

"I was a student of his at Berkeley."

"But Grandfather taught at Stanford."

"Oh, right. Of course. I always get those two confused. I did my undergrad work at one and grad school at the other. At any rate, he was a wonderful professor, a true inspiration."

The woman on the sofa had stopped smiling and was shooting Skyler a funny look.

"This is my fiancée, Jaine Austen," Skyler said, pulling me closer to the action.

His fiancée??

"She wrote 'In a Rush to Flush? Call Toiletmasters!' "

By now, the bereaved granddaughter was eyeing Skyler with outright suspicion. Oh, lord. What if she made a scene and started chewing us out in front of everybody? What if she called the police?

But, thankfully, she said nothing.

"We don't want to take up too much of your time," Skyler said. "There are others waiting to speak with you. All our deepest sympathies."

With that, he took me by the elbow and whisked me away.

When we were alone, I whirled on him.

"Please don't tell me we've just crashed a funeral reception."

"Isn't it great?" he grinned. "Just look at the spread!"

He pointed to a buffet table loaded with cold cuts.

Normally, my taste buds would spring to action at the sight of all this chow, but, apparently, they were just as horrified as I was. I had zero desire to swan dive into the potato salad, as I usually do at buffets. Instead, I just stood there blinking in disbelief.

Skyler's taste buds had no such compunctions.

"I do this all the time," he was saying, making himself a roast beef on rye with cole slaw and thousand island dressing. "I read obits in the paper, and when the funeral is at a high-end cemetery, I show up and find out where the reception's going to be.

"Great," he said, looking around the buffet. "A lull in the action."

Following his gaze, I saw that we were indeed the only two people at the table.

Then, with the sleight of hand of a magician, Skyler whipped out a baggie from his pocket and dumped in a pile of shrimp.

"A snack for later," he said with a wink, slipping the baggie into my new Coach tote. "That's why I always try to bring a date to these things. Easier to walk away with buffet swag."

OMG, I was dating a guy who stole food from funeral receptions!

"You're unbelievable! " I gasped.

"Aw, thanks. Takes a lot of practice. And I don't just do funerals. I do weddings and bar mitzvahs, too!"

That did it.

No way was I spending one more minute with this idiot.

The last thing I saw as I stalked out the door to call an Uber was Skyler shoving cheese puffs in his pocket.

Back home, I gave Skyler's purloined shrimp to Prozac, and—after scrounging around in my cupboards—sat down to a hearty lunch of Triscuits and martini olives.

So much for saying yes to everything.

Chapter Twenty-five

After my visit to Becca, watching her bounce around in her happy bubble, I couldn't stop thinking about how much she had to gain from Misty's death. And how easy it would have been for her to slip in the theater's side door the day of the murder without any of us noticing her.

She was supposedly running errands that day. I remembered bumping into her that morning on her way out of the theater. She'd said she was going to the dentist, then picking up the area rug David wanted for the living room set, and finally going out to a costume-rental shop in Burbank.

If she came back to poison Misty's smoothie, it had to have been some time after lunch and before three PM, when all of us were either onstage or out in the audience.

What if she'd hurried through her errands, finishing them quickly, so she'd have time to race back to the theater for a rendezvous with some rat poison?

I decided to pay a visit to the costume shop in Burbank, the last destination on Becca's To Do list, and do some snooping. But first I had to get the name of the shop. So I called Becca, pretending I needed a costume for a party I'd been invited to.

"How fun!" Becca exclaimed. "What sort of costume party?"

Duh. I should've thought this thing out before I called her.

"Um . . . we're supposed to come dressed as our favorite movie character."

"You don't have to spend money to rent a costume," Becca said. "I can lend you my Princess Leia outfit. I wear it all the time at Comic-Con conventions."

"That's so sweet of you, Becca, but I want to go as . . . as . . ."

Quick, Jaine. Think!

"Margo Channing."

"Who?"

"Margo Channing from the movie *All About Eve*."

"Never heard of it."

That's what I was counting on. I didn't want her offering me a Margo Channing dress she just happened to have in the back of her closet.

At last, she gave me the name of the shop in Burbank, a place called Beverly Hill's Costumes.

I wasn't surprised to learn that Beverly Hill's Costumes was actually in Burbank. That stuff happens a lot here in L.A. Bel Air Plumbing will be in Culver City. Brentwood Auto Parts, in West Covina. And Malibu Sump Pumps, in Pacoima. Businesses are always using fancy locations in their names, even if they're nowhere near their namesake city.

The shop turned out to be a small storefront, crammed with racks of costumes.

I made my way down a narrow aisle past Cinderellas and Draculas to a sales counter in the back, where a hefty woman in a neon-pink wig and floral muumuu sat, reading a copy of the *National Enquirer*. Her makeup looked like it had been slathered on with a trowel, her lips neon-pink to match her wig, her eyelashes so false they could double as feather dusters.

She greeted me with a wide grin, teeth smeared with lipstick.

"Welcome to Beverly Hill's Costumes! I'm Beverly Hill, owner and proprietor."

For the first time, I realized there was an apostrophe in Beverly Hill's Costumes.

"How can I help you?" she asked, still flashing me her lipstick-stained teeth.

"Well . . ." I began.

But before I could say anything else, she was off and running on a hard-sell sales pitch.

"I've got the perfect costume for you," she said, lumbering off her stool and rummaging through one of the racks. "How about this 1920's flapper dress?" She held up a sequined dress covered in fringe. "It just came back yesterday from a movie shoot! Aren't the sequins divine? And that fringe will be perfect for camouflaging your hips," she added, eyeing my hips appraisingly.

Look who's talking, I felt like saying. *You're no runway model in that muumuu.*

"Or how about this!" She whipped out a copy of the iconic white halter dress Marilyn Monroe wore in *The Seven Year Itch*. "Add a pair of white heels and a blond wig, and you're good to go.

"Or this?" she said, reaching for another outfit.

"I'm not here to rent a costume," I finally broke in.

"You want to buy one? Everything here is for sale at a deep discount."

"No, I'm here to ask a few questions."

She eyed me, annoyed, through her feather-duster lashes.

"Well, I'm here to rent costumes, not answer questions," she said, climbing back on her stool behind the counter. "You want answers, go see Madame Rosa, the psychic down the street."

Then she picked up where she'd left off in the *Enquirer*.

Okay, time for plan B.

Rummaging in my purse, I whipped out a USDA Meat Inspector badge I picked up at a flea market ages ago and save for occasions like this.

"Detective Jamison," I said, flashing her the badge. "LAPD."

You'd be surprised how many people don't even look at the badge closely and fall for this bit of trickery.

Sadly, Beverly Hill wasn't one of them.

"Wait a minute," she said grabbing the badge from my hand. "This says USDA Meat Inspector."

"Okay," I confessed, "I'm not with the LAPD. But I am investigating a murder."

"A murder, huh?"

She looked up from her tabloid, interested. Obviously, Bev Hill was a gal who enjoyed a juicy story.

"Do you happen to remember a young woman renting costumes for a production of *I Married a Zombie*?"

"Heck, yes. I couldn't believe they were bringing that clunker back to life."

"It so happens that one of the actors on the production got killed."

"You don't say!" she said eagerly.

"A friend of mine is a suspect in the case, and I'm trying to help him clear his name."

"You are, huh?"

By now, she was definitely interested.

"The gal who came to order costumes for the show: Do you have any idea what time she got here? What time she left?"

"I could always look it up."

"Great!"

"For a paying customer," she added with a sly smile. "Not for someone just pretending to be a cop."

"Okay," I sighed, reaching for a Frankenstein mask on display at the counter. "How much to rent this?"

"Forty bucks."

Was she kidding? I could *buy* a mask for half that price! But I'd driven all the way out here, and I wasn't about to throw in the towel. Reluctantly, I forked over two twenties.

"Let me see what I can find," Bev said, once our transaction was complete.

She opened a drawer behind the counter, stuffed with a mountain of credit-card merchant copies, and began rifling through them.

Oh, hell. She'd never find Becca's receipt in all that mess.

But, miraculously, she did.

"Here it is!" she said waving the receipt. "From I Married a Zombie Productions. Time of purchase: One twenty-seven PM. I remember her clearly now. Mousy gal with bangs in her eyes. She seemed to be in a big rush. Said she had a very important chore she had to take care of."

Bingo!

If Becca left the costume shop at around 1:30, she could have easily been back at the theater in time to slip some rat poison in Misty's smoothie.

Of course, it's quite possible the chore Becca had to take care of was perfectly innocent. Like getting her bangs trimmed. Or her car serviced. Or checking out a sale on Cryptessa bobbleheads.

Then again, maybe that final item on her To Do list was bumping off the bimbo who was ruining her life.

Chapter Twenty-six

Lemme outta here!

Prozac was clawing at the front door, clamoring to go for a walk.

But no way was I about to let her loose on my street and risk a repeat performance of the paw-prints-on-a-Mercedes incident.

I had to take her somewhere, though, before she clawed my front door to splinters. But where? And then the answer came to me: A park! How much damage could she possibly do running around on a patch of grass?

Feeling quite proud of myself, I strapped her into her harness, attached the leash, and headed for my Corolla.

I left her detested cat carrier behind, unwilling to endure the godawful racket she makes every time I put her in it. Instead I wrapped her leash around the passenger seat headrest, giving her just enough room to sit on the seat, but tight enough to keep her from prancing around the pedals as she's so fond of doing when I'm driving.

And it worked. I'm happy to say she went nowhere near the pedals.

Instead, she focused her energy on ripping a hole in my passenger seat.

It was a picture-postcard day as I drove over to Roxbury Gardens, a park not far from my duplex. Fluffy clouds scudded across a sapphire sky, the temperature somewhere in Los Angeles's ever-popular seventies.

After finding a spot for my Corolla, I made my way to the park, carrying Prozac in my arms, keeping her and her paws away from any parked cars.

We arrived at the entrance to the park, a grassy oasis dotted with shade trees, picnic tables, and benches along paved walkways. I set Prozac down, the handle of her leash looped around my wrist, and watched as she eagerly began attacking an ant unlucky enough to be strolling by.

Looking around, I saw men playing chess, couples smooching on the benches, families chowing down at the picnic tables, still others lolling on blankets on the grass.

But the most entrancing sight of all was a vendor selling soft drinks and giant pretzels.

I quickly snapped up a pretzel and an orange soda.

(My idea of fun in the great outdoors.)

Then I found a nice shady spot under a tree, where I plopped down, sitting on the handle of Prozac's leash to free up my hands so I could enjoy my snack.

Prozac was in seventh heaven, scampering around as far as the leash would allow, terrorizing squirrels, birds, large dogs, and senior citizens.

I, too, was a mighty happy camper. It had been ages since I'd had a giant pretzel, and I'd forgotten how yummy they were. I was thinking how delicious it would be as a sandwich, sliced down the middle and stuffed with pastrami and Swiss cheese, when I took a closer look at one of the couples playing kissy-face on the benches. There was something about the guy's skinny bod and mop of wiry hair that looked familiar.

Wait a second. Was that David?

The smoochers were partially obscured by a tree, and I

couldn't see the woman he was kissing. When they finally broke apart, I stood up to get a better look.

Yep, the guy was David, all right. But the woman he'd been kissing was not Becca.

Not even close. She was a hot young blonde in cutoffs and a tank top.

So David was getting it on with another hottie. First, Misty. Now Blondie.

So much for his "Woe is me, I'm a broken man" act. And so much for his devotion to Becca. The guy was a player. A cheat. A nogoodnik. Quite capable, I thought, of killing a lover who'd humiliated him.

Just as I was thinking what a louse he was, I became aware of people shouting. I looked around to see what the fuss was about and saw a crowd gathered underneath a tall oak tree.

"That poor cat!" I heard an elderly woman cry. "It's trapped up there."

Dammit. In my eagerness to get a look at David and his smooch partner, I'd jumped up from where I'd been sitting on Prozac's leash.

I raced over to the tree, and sure enough, there she was, high up in the branches, yowling her heart out.

People below were tsking in sympathy.

"Poor little darling," someone was saying. "Look how frightened she is."

Prozac, frightened? No way. That cat thrives on being the center of attention. She was loving every minute of this, hamming it up for an appreciative audience.

"She can't get down!" another bystander cried in dismay.

Oh, please. That cat could scamper down Mount Everest if there were a kitty treat at the bottom.

Now I heard a siren wailing. Someone had called the fire department. Soon an eye-poppingly handsome fireman, fresh off a World's Sexiest Firefighters calendar, was on the scene, setting up a ladder against the tree to "rescue" Prozac.

As he made his way up the ladder, Prozac amped up her yowls, turning in a virtuoso performance for the hunky firefighter.

When he finally reached the branch she was perched on, he did not have to coax Prozac to come closer, as he would've had to do with a cat who was truly frightened. Instead, my shameless hussy leaped into his arms.

I could practically hear her purring from where I stood. *Hubba hubba, hot stuff!*

Everyone applauded as the fireman made his way back down the ladder with Pro.

"Who does this cat belong to?" the fireman asked when he was back on the ground.

"Um, that would be me." I stepped forward timidly.

All around me, the crowd murmured their disapproval.

"What kind of irresponsible cat owner lets go of her adorable kitty's leash?"

"Some people shouldn't be allowed to own pets."

"We ought to report her to the ASPCA."

The adorable kitty in question was now nuzzling the fireman's neck with wild abandon.

"You need to take better care of your cat," said Prozac's rugged rescuer.

"I'm so sorry," I sputtered. "I'm afraid I got a bit distracted."

"As a pet owner, you can't afford to get distracted," he chided, giving me the stink eye.

A chorus of amens from the angry crowd. Any minute now, I expected one of them to come after me with a pitchfork.

Reluctantly the fireman handed me Prozac, who wailed in protest.

Wait a minute! I'm not finished nuzzling his neck! Then I was going to give him a lap dance! I thought I'd go home with him and spend the night!

"Look!" cried one of the angry mob. "The cat doesn't even want to go back to her."

"We really should report her to the ASPCA."

With Prozac wailing in my arms, I promised the fireman I'd take better care of my kitty, then hustled out of the park, everyone glaring at me.

I can't tell you how upset I was. Especially since I never got to finish my giant pretzel.

"I hope you're proud of yourself, young lady," I hissed at Prozac as soon as we were back on the street.

A satisfied meow.

Very! Did you see how everybody paid attention to me? I was a star!

"You embarrassed me in front of all those people!"

That was certainly an added bonus!

"If you think I'm taking you for any more walks, you're sadly mistaken."

I continued chewing her out, telling her in no uncertain terms what a traitorous ingrate she was. Unfortunately, she heard none of it, as she'd launched into one of her power naps.

Nevertheless, I continued my rant, and I was in the middle of threatening to trade her in for a gerbil when suddenly someone grabbed my shoulder roughly from behind.

At first, I thought it was one of the angry mob from the park, but I was wrong.

It was David.

In the hooha of Prozac's treescapade, I'd forgotten all about him.

Now he yanked me around to face him, glowering at me, jaw clenched, the veins in his neck throbbing.

"I caught you watching me at the park."

I didn't like the look of those throbbing veins, but I wasn't about to be intimidated.

"Yes, I see you've recovered quite nicely from the trauma of Misty's death."

"You'd better not tell Becca what you saw. She's a good producer, and I can't afford to lose her. Not until the show opens on Broadway, anyway. Then I'll let her go."

What a ghastly guy. And that sad sack routine at rehearsals was just an act, too—letting us think he didn't care about the play. He was every bit as invested in his production as he'd been when we first met. Maybe even more so. And certainly capable, in my humble op, of killing Misty.

I had no intention of telling Becca what I'd seen in the park. She'd learn the ugly truth about David sooner or later. But I wasn't going to be the one to break her heart.

Now he grabbed my shoulder again, squeezing it in a viselike grip.

For a skinny guy, he was surprisingly strong.

"This is the last time I'm going to warn you, Jaine. Mind your own business."

Then he turned on his heel and stalked off.

Shoulder aching from where he'd grabbed me, I hustled to my car.

I won't deny it, I was spooked.

On the drive home, I couldn't help wondering what David meant when he said, "This is the last time I'm going to warn you."

The last time? Had he warned me before? Was it possible this cheating lothario was the one who'd scared me half to death with that bloody headstone in the theater?

By the time I got home, David had once again vaulted to the top of my suspect list.

Meanwhile, Prozac, my ever-vigilant protector, was still snoring like a buzz saw. She'd slept clear through my frightening encounter with a probable killer.

I really had to look into that gerbil thing.

Chapter Twenty-seven

"**M**ore shrimp with lobster sauce?" Aidan asked.

"I really shouldn't," I said, scooping some out of the carton.

Aidan had invited Lance and me to his place that night so I could give them a progress report on the murder. He'd ordered Chinese food for dinner—shrimp with lobster sauce, chicken lo mein, wonton soup, and potstickers.

"Shrimp with lobster sauce is my favorite!" I exclaimed.

"Mine too!" said Aidan.

"Mine too!" Lance chimed in.

Really? This from the guy who, whenever he saw me eating the stuff, sneered, "Do you realize how many calories there are in that goop?"

But now, in front of Aidan, he was a poster boy for shrimp with lobster sauce, eating it with fake gusto, probably calculating the number of calories he'd have to burn off at the gym.

We were seated in the dining alcove of Aidan's surprisingly upscale condo in Venice. "I do some modeling on the side to pay the bills," he'd explained when I'd looked around in awe at his hardwood floors, recessed lighting, and sleek West Elm-ish furniture.

"So tell us what's happening with your investigation, Jaine."

Reluctantly I tore myself away from my shrimp to fill them in on what I'd learned since our last confab.

I started with the bombshell about Misty being responsible for Delia's sister's death, and how Delia might have killed her in the ultimate act of revenge. Then I told them about Becca's hasty exit from Beverly Hill's costume shop to take care of an "important chore." And about Misty's angry ex-boyfriend, who'd been tracking Misty with a phone app, and how he could have slipped in the side door of the theater to do away with his cheating ex. And how Katie might have used that very same side door to kill for a part she was desperate to get.

Finally, I told them about David, how his post-murder grief was just an act, how I'd caught him smooching with a young hottie and cheating on Becca, and how I suspected him of luring me to the theater and scaring me half to death with a bloody headstone.

"Right now," I said, reaching for a potsticker, "my money's on David."

"Wow," Aidan said. "You've done a great job digging up suspects."

"Too bad I don't have any evidence linking any of them to the murder."

"The episode at the theater with the bloody headstone sounds pretty dangerous," Aidan said. "I'm thinking maybe you should give up your investigation. I don't want you getting hurt."

"I still say it's a mob hit," Lance piped up, eager to step into the spotlight.

Not that stupid theory again!

"In fact, I've done some research online and read about

a guy named Al 'The Jawbreaker' Buono getting bumped off with poison, just like Misty. Only in The Jawbreaker's case, they used antifreeze."

"I dunno, Lance," I said. "Misty was an unscrupulous bitch, but not exactly a rocket scientist. She couldn't even remember Cryptessa's one-sentence speeches. I can't picture her coordinating a bunch of drug deals."

"Jaine has a point," said Aidan.

"Maybe," Lance grudgingly conceded, but only because he was toadying up to Aidan, unwilling to disagree with him on anything except possibly which flowers to order for their wedding.

"I just hope the killer isn't Katie," Aidan said. "She's terrific in the play."

"Not nearly as good as you," Lance gushed. "I stopped in at rehearsals the other day," he added, turning to me. "Aidan was stealing the show as Uncle Dedly. And I'm not just saying that because I'm madly in love with the guy and want to boink him."

No, he didn't say that last part. He didn't have to, not the way he was mooning over Aidan like a mutt at the pound hoping to get adopted.

"Time for fortune cookies!" Aidan announced, passing us each a cookie.

Lance opened his eagerly, and read: *The fortune you seek is in another cookie.*

He frowned at the piece of paper in his hand. "Wait, what?"

"They're comedy fortune cookies," Aidan explained with a laugh. "This restaurant specializes in them. Mine says, *Help! I'm a prisoner in a fortune cookie factory.*

"What about yours, Jaine?"

"You've got rice in your teeth."

Aidan and I chuckled, but Lance was clearly miffed that he hadn't been promised true love and a lifetime supply of Ferragamos.

By now, the wonton soup and excellent chardonnay we'd been drinking had coursed through my system, and I excused myself to use Aidan's bathroom.

"It's down the hall to your left," he said.

After a quick tinkle, admiring Aidan's glass-enclosed shower with multiple showerheads, I started back down the hallway, but stopped when I saw the door to Aidan's bedroom was open. I couldn't resist taking a peek inside.

(What can I say? You know how nosy I am.)

Like the living room, the bedroom was sleek and modern. Floating shelves flanked both sides of his bed, while a flat-screen TV was mounted on the opposite wall.

I wandered over to the floating shelves and smiled at Aidan's collection of kitschy cartoon-character snow globes. Scattered among the snow globes were photos of Aidan with friends at the beach, with an older couple I assumed were his parents, and in front of the La Brea Tar Pits with his arm around the shoulder of a handsome hunk of a guy. (I knew Lance wasn't going to like that last one.)

Then I came across a picture of a chubby, pimply teenager with sad eyes and ears too big for his head. With a jolt of surprise, I realized it was Aidan.

"Yep, that's me," Aidan said, "before my acne meds kicked in."

I turned to see him standing in the doorway.

"I keep it framed on my shelf to remind myself that no matter how tough things get, my life is so much better now than it was then."

"Gosh, I'm sorry," I said, flustered at having been caught snooping. "I didn't mean to pry."

Then, in my eagerness to put the photo back on the shelf, I accidentally knocked over an Elmer Fudd snow globe and sent it rolling under Aidan's bed.

"Oh, no!" I said, hurrying to retrieve it.

"I'll get that!" Aidan said, racing to my side.

But I was already on my knees lifting the bedspread when I saw something else under the bed—one of the prop headstones from the play. A wave of dread washed over me as I pulled it out and saw the spray-painted words RIP JAINE AUSTEN.

It was the same headstone that had given me heart palpitations at the theater.

Omigosh. It was Aidan who'd set out to terrorize me that night. Could it be? Was Aidan the killer?

When I turned to look at him, however, he didn't seem very homicidal—just red-faced and sheepish.

"I've been meaning to clean off the graffiti, but I haven't gotten around to it yet."

"So it was you who lured me to the theater?"

"Yes," he admitted, "but I only meant to scare you, to stop your investigation."

"But why? I was only trying to help."

With a sigh, he went to his closet and brought back a high school yearbook.

"Here I am fourteen years ago at Fresno High." He pointed to a thumbnail photo of the same acne-ridden Aidan he had framed on his shelf. Then he flipped to another page, where one of the photos had been defaced. In spite of the bold Sharpie "X" slashed across the picture, I recognized the deceptively elfin face.

It was Misty.

"We went to the same high school, and she made my life—along with plenty of others—a living hell. She took real pleasure in tormenting us. She didn't recognize me when we met at the theater. But I remembered her all right. I was so repulsed when she came on to me backstage, I wanted to shove her through the scenery."

He grimaced at the memory.

"I was hoping the police wouldn't discover we'd known each other in the past. And as far as I know, they haven't. But I was afraid you might."

"Me?" I blinked, puzzled.

"Remember that day you stopped by the theater to question Delia? You and I were chatting, and you said something about Misty being a mean girl in high school, how she probably tortured the unpopular kids. And I panicked. I thought somehow you'd make the connection and discover how much I loathed her. So I tried to scare you off with this stupid headstone stunt."

He gave the headstone a desultory kick.

"But I didn't kill Misty. Honest. I hated her guts, but I didn't kill her."

"Of course, Aidan didn't kill Misty!" Lance cried, rushing into the bedroom. "You don't really suspect him, do you?"

And I had to confess that at that moment Aidan looked singularly angelic, a cross between an altar boy and a Calvin Klein underwear model.

"No, of course not," I said.

But I wasn't really sure.

True, Aidan was the picture of innocence. But as with so many of the players in this little drama, I had no idea if it was just a finely honed performance.

For all I knew, Lance's heartthrob and my secret crush was a shrimp-with-lobster-sauce-loving killer.

Chapter Twenty-eight

I got a welcome break from the murder the next morning when Susie Pearson of the Pasadena Historical Society called.

"Sorry for the last-minute invitation," she said, "but the board of directors is meeting for lunch today, and we'd love to have you join us. The other gals on the board want to meet you before we officially offer you the position as our PR writer."

Yes! I was that much closer to landing the job. Not to mention a free lunch.

"I'd be delighted," I said, hoping I'd find steak on the menu.

I hung up in a happy glow and turned to Prozac, who was power napping on my sofa.

"Guess what, Pro? I'm having lunch with the Pasadena Historical Society. I may get that plum job after all!"

She opened a sleepy eye and thumped her tail, irritated.

One of these days, I've got to get myself a Do Not Disturb sign.

I gave her a love scratch she didn't deserve and hurried off to find something appropriate to wear for my meetup with the Pasadena doyennes. I was surveying the contents of my closet, wishing I had fewer sweatpants and a lot more Ladies Who Lunch outfits, when I heard a loud banging at my front door.

It was Lance, looking none too happy.

"I can't believe you suspect Aidan of murder!" he cried, stomping into my apartment. "Just when I finally meet my one true love, you're trying to ruin things."

Puh-leese. Lance meets his one true love as often as he gets his highlights done.

"Cool your jets, Lance. I don't suspect Aidan of murder."

Which wasn't exactly true. I was still haunted by the memory of that headstone under his bed.

But I was never going to get rid of Lance unless I fibbed.

"Honest, Lance. I'm sure Aidan's innocent. Now you've really got to run along. I need to get dressed for a very important job interview."

"I don't suppose you noticed that picture of Aidan with his ex-boyfriend last night," he said, plopping down on my sofa. "The one at the La Brea Tar Pits."

Aack! How annoying. The man can hear my refrigerator humming from his bedroom, but he's tone deaf when he wants to be.

I did indeed remember the photo of Aidan with his arm slung around the shoulder of a handsome honey. But I had zero time to discuss it.

"Aidan insists they're just friends," Lance was saying, scooping Prozac into his lap for a belly rub. "But I'm not sure I believe him. You think there's any chance he's still into him?"

"No! None whatsoever. Now you've got to go so I can get dressed."

"I dunno," Lance said, still welded to my sofa. "Why

would he have that picture on his shelf if he weren't still in love with him?"

"Because they're just friends. End of story. You've got nothing to worry about."

He looked up at me, hopeful.

"You really think so?"

"I know so!' I said, prying Prozac from his lap.

She shot me an angry glare.

Hey, wait! He wasn't through rubbing my belly!

"Omigosh," Lance said, jumping up. "Look at the time. If I don't hurry, I'll be late for my spin class. And look at you! Eleven AM and you're still in your pjs. Don't you think it's about time you got dressed?"

And off he sailed, holding on to his title as the world's most aggravating man.

Alone at last, I raced to the bathroom for a quickie shower, then chose my outfit for my luncheon with the bluebloods. I went with a cashmere sweater and tailored slacks with a set-in waistband. Yes, I know set-in waistbands are nature's torture chambers, but that's how much I wanted the gig. No way could these fancy ladies see elastic clinging to my bod.

I accessorized with a string of pearls and my new Coach tote. When I was done, I surveyed myself in the mirror. Pleased with what I saw, I headed back out to the living room.

"I'm off to lunch!" I called out to Pro, still lolling on the sofa. "Wish me luck!"

She responded with a cavernous yawn.

Don't forget to bring back leftovers.

Grabbing my purse, I hurried out to my Corolla for my trek to Pasadena.

The drive was a slog, but I didn't mind. I was too excited thinking about my prestigious job in the offing, not to mention that free lunch.

I arrived at my destination, the historic Huntington Hotel, a majestic affair with a soaring tower and massive wings that gave Buckingham Palace a run for its money.

When I left my car keys with the valet, he looked like I'd just handed him a particularly slimy cockroach. But I didn't care. Determined to think positive, I strode into the hotel, my head held high. I couldn't help but feel a tad awed, though, when I entered the lobby and saw its eye-popping chandeliers, marble floors, and straight outta Versailles furniture.

Then, as I stowed my valet parking stub in my purse, I noticed a funny smell. A faint whiff of rotting garbage. How odd, for such a fancy place. I figured their ventilation system was on the fritz.

I made my way to the main dining room, where I was greeted by a maître d' with the aristocratic air of an exiled European nobleman.

When I told him I was with the Pasadena Historical Society, he led me out onto a sun-dappled patio, a heavenly oasis of linen-clad tables, potted palms, and fresh-cut freesias.

I recognized Susie Pearson from our Zoom chat. She waved me over to a round table where four other women and an elderly gent were already seated.

I had trouble telling the women apart, all conservatively dressed in what looked like Chanel suits, their various shades of ash-blond hair carefully coiffed, some caught up in headbands. The kind of bluebloods who look down at Mayflower descendants as riffraff.

The only giveaway of their wealth were the rocklike diamonds flashing on their fingers.

As I took a seat, Susie went around the table, telling me their names, the kind of goofy prep school monikers favored by the upper crust. For the purposes of this narrative, let's call them Bitsy, Betsy, Muffy, and Buffy.

The elderly gent, named Ward, dressed in a seersucker suit, gazed at me appreciatively with rheumy eyes and a martini clenched firmly in his fist.

"Everybody, meet Jaine Austen!" Susie said with a flourish.

The women smiled politely, while Ward shot me a suggestive wink.

"Jaine Austen?" said Bitsy. (Or Betsy; it was really hard to tell these gals apart.) "Any relation to the famous author?"

"Very distant," I replied.

Holy moly, where had that come from? No way was I related to the real Jane Austen, but I'd been so eager to make a good impression, it came barreling out of my mouth before I could stop myself.

"Really?" cried Bitsy/Betsy. "Me too! My great-great-great-great-grandmother was Jane Austen's cousin. What about you?"

Oh, dear. I couldn't keep this lie going. The last thing I needed was for one of them to ask me to whip out my family tree.

"It's probably apocryphal," I said. "Just something Grandpa Austen used to say at Thanksgiving dinner, after a bit too much wine."

Then one of the gals, it may have been Muffy (or Buffy), dressed a tad flashier than the others, with a diamond ring the size of a golf ball, sniffed the air and frowned.

"Is it my imagination, or does something smell bad out here?"

It wasn't her imagination. I still smelled that funky smell from the lobby. I thought for sure it would be gone outside, but it wasn't.

"Yes, you're right," echoed one of the others. "It smells positively rank."

Then, to my horror, Bitsy/Betsy turned to me and said, "I think it's coming from your handbag."

My new Coach tote? Impossible!

But when I opened it to peek inside, I realized she was right. It smelled like a sewer in there. Rifling through the contents, I finally discovered the culprit—a decomposing shrimp, stuck in the corner of my bag.

Lord, no! I flashed back on the shrimp Skyler had tossed in my purse the day of the funeral reception. I thought I'd dumped them all out when I got home, but apparently this one critter had escaped my notice.

"I found the problem," I said, jumping up from the table. "I'll go take care of it."

"Hurry back, June!" Ward said, with a wink, as I raced off to find the ladies' room.

The maître d' gave me directions, and soon I was standing at a white marble sink dumping my shrimp in the trash. A gray-haired matron washing her hands next to me wrinkled her nose in disgust and scooted out as fast as she could. As soon as she left, I emptied the contents of my purse on the counter and flapped my purse around, trying to air it out. It helped a little, but I could still smell that darn eau de shrimp.

I couldn't go back to the table with my purse in this condition. So, after shoving its contents back inside, I dashed out of the ladies' room on a frantic search for the gift shop. I finally found it at the end of a corridor lined with overpriced boutiques and forked over an outrageous amount of money for a travel-size spray can of deodorant. Which I spritzed lavishly in my purse.

At last, I got rid of the noxious odor and hurried to rejoin the others on the patio.

"Welcome back, June!" Ward cried when I got back to the table.

Alas, he was the only one who seemed happy to see me.

"What was that ghastly smell?" asked Muffy/Buffy as I slid back into my seat.

"A shrimp," I admitted.

"A shrimp? What on earth was a shrimp doing in your purse?"

I couldn't tell them the truth, that it was filched from a funeral reception.

"I was eating a shrimp taco the other day, and you know how messy those things are. I guess a piece of shrimp fell into my purse."

"I don't find shrimp tacos the least bit messy," Bitsy/Betsy said.

"And I've never had any fall into my purse," echoed Muffy/Buffy.

"What's a shrimp taco?" Ward asked.

"So, Jaine," Susie said, eager to change the subject. "What would you like for lunch?"

In my dismay over the whole shrimp debacle, I'd forgotten about my free meal. I picked up the menu and was buoyed to see petite filet mignon listed as an entree. I wasn't crazy about the petite part, but I was all in for the filet mignon.

And I was just about to say so when Bitsy/Betsy piped up, "I highly recommend the kale caesar salad. That's what we're all getting."

"I'm getting another martini," Ward said, with yet another wink.

Phooey. I couldn't possibly order a steak, not when they were all ordering kale salads.

What was it with L.A.'s obsession with kale salads anyway? If you ask me, whoever decided that kale was fit for human consumption was probably the same sadistic devil who came up with set-in waistbands.

For a nanosecond, I'd been tempted to throw caution to the winds and order the steak, but in the end I chickened out.

"Kale salad!" I said, plastering a smile on my face. "Sounds yum. I'll have that, too."

I'd pretty much given up any hopes of getting the job when Susie Pearson threw me what turned out to be a lifeline.

"Jaine, tell us how you became interested in the architectural history of Pasadena."

Taking a deep breath, I started telling the gals what I'd told Susie on our Zoom chat: How I'd always loved Pasadena's great old Victorian and Craftsman homes, how I'd been on many an architectural tour, and how I liked to imagine what life must have been like at the turn of the twentieth century, soon after Pasadena first sprang up, one of L.A.'s oldest and toniest suburbs.

If I do say so myself, I was pretty darn eloquent.

The ladies were now looking at me with newfound respect.

"See?" said Susie. "I told you she'd be perfect for the job!"

The others murmured their assent—some even broke out in a smile—and Ward blew me a kiss.

It looked like I'd overcome the stigma of Shrimp-gate. Yay, me!

When our disgusting kale salads showed up, I didn't

even care that I was missing out on a steak. (Okay, maybe I cared. But only a little.)

I could always fill up on bread. A basket of fresh-from-the-oven rolls had been delivered to our table, along with Ward's umpteenth martini.

Eagerly, I reached for one of the golden beauties. And as I did, Muffy/Buffy, the one with the golf ball–size ring, let out a shriek.

"My ring!" she said, reaching across the table to grab my hand. "That's the emerald-and-diamond ring my husband bought me for my last birthday."

I looked down at the ring on my finger—another memento from the infamous All You Can Eat Funeral Buffet, the ring I thought Skyler picked up at the 99 Cent Store.

Could it be? Was this colorful piece of costume jewelry actually real?

Apparently so.

"It's my ring all right," Muffy/Buffy cried, ripping it off my finger. "Here's the inscription inside the band. *To Muffy/Buffy from Skip.*"

I'd put it on this morning without even giving it a second thought. No wonder I liked it. The damn thing was real.

"I lost it in a limo weeks ago!" Muffy/Buffy was saying.

Darn that Skyler! He must've found it in his limo and, not realizing its worth, tossed it in the trunk with the rest of his limo loot.

"How on earth did you get it?" Bitsy/Betsy asked.

"Someone gave it to me as a gift. I had no idea it was real. I thought it was costume jewelry."

Now they were all staring at me much like the valet had stared at my Corolla. I was pretty sure they thought I was part of a jewelry-fencing ring.

"I think maybe I'd better go," I said, sizing up the zeitgeist of the table.

"Perhaps it would be for the best," Susie said softly.

I got up from my seat and headed back into the hotel with as much pride as I could muster.

Oh, well. I had to look on the bright side. At least I didn't have to eat that damn kale salad.

You've Got Mail

To: Jausten
From: DaddyO
Subject: The Show Must Go On!

Tonight's the big night, Lambchop. Time for the Tampa Vistas talent show. I'm sad to say that Iggy is still missing, and it won't be the same without him. But nonetheless, I intend to tap-dance my way to victory!

Love 'n snuggles,
Daddy

To: Jausten
From: Shoptillyoudrop

We're off to the talent show—without Iggy, thank goodness. At least I'll be spared the embarrassment of watching Daddy tap-dance with an iguana on his head.

XOXO,
Mom

Tampa Vistas Gazette

Leaping Lizards!
Iguana terrorizes Tampa Vistas residents

To: Jausten
From: Shoptillyoudrop
Subject: Utter Fiasco

The talent show was an utter fiasco! The worst ever!

Of course, I had no idea of the disaster to come when I took my seat in the audience last night. It was a full house—packed with Tampa Vistas residents, their children and grandchildren. Projected onto a big screen at the back of the stage were the words:

Welcome to the Tampa Vistas Talent Show—Where Senior Stars Come to Shine!

It was all going so well at first. Nick Roulakis wowed everyone with his harmonica rendition of "Lady of Spain." And Edna Lindstrom got lots of appreciative laughs performing the balcony scene from *Romeo and Juliet* with her hand puppets. The star of the evening, of course, was Lydia Pinkus, who really is a virtuoso on her violin. I'm surprised she hasn't been snapped up by a world-famous symphony orchestra.

In all the fun of watching the acts, I'd almost forgotten about Daddy. But then they announced his name, and he came strutting onstage in his tux and tap shoes, twirling a cane.

After dedicating his dance to his "beloved Iggy," he started in on his routine. I just hoped he'd be able to get through it without tripping over his own feet. That wish was granted. (Although he did manage to trip over his cane a few times.)

A wave of relief washed over me as I realized he wasn't going to make a complete fool of himself. Then, just as I was beginning to relax, the poop hit the fan.

Daddy was almost through with his act when the shadow of a huge reptilian creature appeared on the screen behind him. Someone in the audience screamed, "Look! It's Godzilla!" And indeed the shadow creeping across the stage looked a lot like the famous movie monster. The grandkids began crying. Even the adults were scared watching the creature's shadow lumber across the stage. Before long, everyone was screaming and running for the exits.

Lydia had the presence of mind to call 911, and when the police arrived they found Iggy in the projection room. Apparently, he'd gotten out of the house and had been roaming around Tampa Vistas. (I knew all along Daddy hadn't latched his cage properly!)

Somehow, he'd wandered over to the clubhouse, found his way into the projection booth, and strolled in front of the projector, which blew up his shadow to terrifying proportions.

So instead of enjoying a fun evening, everyone wound up huddled in the parking lot, grandparents explaining to their bawling grandchildren that the "monster" they saw was just an iguana.

What a shambles! All thanks to Daddy.

I may never speak to him again!

XOXO,
Mom

To: Jausten
From: DaddyO
Subject: Surprise Cameo

I suppose Mom's told you about Iggy's surprise cameo appearance at the talent show. I can't understand why everyone got so freaked out. If you ask me, his was the best performance of the night.

Not only have I been unfairly banned from the clubhouse for six months, but now Mom's not speaking to me. I'm going to have to do some serious groveling to get back in her good graces.

Wish me luck, Lambchop!

Love 'n munches
From your despondent
Daddy

Chapter Twenty-nine

Reeling from the humiliation of my stinky purse and ill-gotten ring—not to mention the twelve bucks I had to pay for valet parking—I left the Pasadena bluebloods and drove over to the nearest McDonald's. The Big Mac and fries I ordered, which normally have my taste buds jumping for joy, were like sawdust in my mouth.

I was so upset, I couldn't even finish them.

To make a bad day worse, I checked my emails and read about Iggy's cameo appearance as Godzilla at the Tampa Vistas talent show. What did I tell you about Daddy? A FEMA-grade disaster magnet!

And, to top things off, the freeways were a parking lot. It took me almost two hours to slog my way from Pasadena back to my apartment. I whiled away the time cursing Skyler and, if you must know, polishing off my burger and fries.

After all, I had to do *something* to pass the time.

Back home, I made a beeline for the bathtub—my sanctuary in times of crisis, the place I go to de-stress and find inner peace. Before long, I was up to my neck in strawberry-scented bubbles, as Prozac perched across from me on the toilet tank, giving herself a thorough gynecological exam.

"Oh, Pro," I moaned. "What a nightmare!"

I proceeded to tell her about the shrimp in my purse, and how, thanks to Skyler, I got caught wearing Muffy/ Buffy's honker emerald-and-diamond ring and didn't even get to stay for lunch.

"You know what this means, don't you?"

She looked up from her privates.

Yeah. No leftovers.

"It means I've lost my chance at my dream job, that I'll probably be writing toilet bowl ads for the rest of my life."

Reluctantly, Prozac tore herself away from her privates.

And this matters to me because . . . ?

I should've known not to expect empathy from the cat who put the "me" in "meow."

So I continued to soak in the steamy suds, trying to visualize soothing, restful images: A beach at sunset. A palm tree swaying in the breeze. A sausage and pepperoni pizza dripping with gooey cheese . . .

Bingo!

Just the thought of that pizza sent the stress draining from my bod. I'd definitely have to order one for dinner. With extra sausage for even more inner peace.

My muscles now the consistency of limp linguini, I dredged myself out of the tub and slipped into a pair of jammies, then nestled under the covers in bed for a quickie nap. Twenty minutes max.

Two hours later, I was jarred awake by my phone.

"Jaine, where are you?" Becca's voice came over the line. "The party's already started."

"Party?"

"The 'Come as a Zombie' costume party."

Right. Becca's ghoulish gala, where everyone was supposed to wear zombie capes. I'd forgotten all about it.

"You haven't forgotten, have you?"

"Of course not. I was just getting ready to leave."

"Well, hurry! You're missing all the fun. The plastic capes I ordered online turned out to be really cute, and I'm saving a red one for you."

"Great! See you soon."

I hung up with a sigh.

So much for my inner-peace pizza.

When I showed up at the theater, the party was in full swing, people milling around onstage in hooded capes. The actors wore long dramatic numbers from Bev Hill's Costume Shop, while everyone else wore the plastic capes Becca had ordered online. Several Cryptessa enthusiasts had come in zombie makeup, blood smeared across unnaturally ashen faces.

Meanwhile, in the background, eerie moans, groans, and screams were being piped in over the sound system.

I spotted Becca in a white cape, her bangs peeking out from under the hood, chatting with a guy in full zombie regalia.

"Hey, Jaine," she said, as she saw me climbing up the steps to the stage. "Here's your cape."

It was actually more of a poncho than a cape. I figured it would come in handy during L.A.'s twelve-and-a-half-day rainy season.

"Meet Zack Brenner," she said, introducing me to the skinny nerdling she'd been chatting with. "Zack writes the *Cryptessa-Mania* blog. It's very popular."

"I've got a hundred and twenty-seven followers!" he boasted.

Yikes. There were Trappist monks in Siberia with more followers than this guy.

"It's so fantastic that you're bringing Cryptessa back to

life!" he said to Becca, eyes wide with enthusiasm. "I can't wait to see the play!"

Don't get your hopes up, I felt like telling him.

"Catch you later," he said and headed off to chat with a fellow nerdling.

"I invited everyone from the *I Married a Zombie* fan club," Becca said. Indeed, the crowd was an eclectic mix of *I Married a Zombie* geeks and well-heeled show biz types, no doubt friends of the actors.

"And there's one of our influencers." Becca pointed to a goth gal with a jet-black mohawk and multiple hoops in her ears, busy taking selfies with one of the prop headstones.

I only hoped she had more followers than Zack.

Just then Katie came sailing up to us, her Bev Hill's cape flaring dramatically in her wake.

"What a great turnout!" she said, surveying the partygoers.

"I know!" Becca cried. "Isn't it terrific?"

"You did a wonderful job organizing everything," Katie said, giving Becca a hug. "And I loved your press release," she added, turning to me.

"Well, I'd better go work the crowd. Cryptessa's blood may not be circulating, but I sure intend to."

And off she went to hype the play.

"Katie's been such an asset to the show," Becca said.

"Not half as much of an asset as you, hon."

I turned to see David sidling up to Becca, placing a possessive arm around her waist.

She smiled up at him, starry-eyed.

Poor trusting Becca. If she only knew the truth about her lowlife creep of a boyfriend.

"Nice to see you, Jaine," David said, giving me the stink eye.

I remembered how angry he'd been that day at the park, how roughly he'd yanked me by the shoulder and warned me to mind my own business.

In spite of the frisson of fear running down my spine, I managed to lob his stink eye right back at him.

"Help yourself to some hors d'oeuvres," Becca said brightly, perhaps sensing the tension in the air. She pointed to a buffet table at the rear of the stage.

I didn't have to be asked twice.

"Thanks, I will."

And off I hustled to the buffet. In my humble op, it was the hit of the party, a veritable carbo heaven, laden with platters of franks-in-a-blanket, bagel bites, and pizza pockets.

I was just popping a frank-in-a-blanket in my mouth when I saw Aidan, decked out in his black Uncle Dedly cape, waving at me from behind a makeshift bar across the stage. Somehow I managed to pry myself away from the buffet to go over and say hello.

Two pretty young things—one blonde, one brunette—in skintight dresses were at the bar, snapping pics of themselves, grinning and holding Bloody Marys. As soon as they turned off their cameras, they turned off their smiles.

"What a bunch of losers," the blonde said, looking around. "And those cheap plastic ponchos. Ugh. I wouldn't be caught dead in them."

"Let's stick it out for another fifteen minutes and make tracks," said the brunette.

Then they turned to Aidan.

"Want to ditch this mess," the blonde asked, flirting outrageously, "and come to a real party?"

"Thanks, but I'm actually part of this mess. I'm in the play."

"Poor you," they clucked in unison.

As they wandered off, Aidan shook his head in disgust. "Influencers. Ugh. I wonder how much money Becca's wasted on them."

"Too much, I'm sure."

We smiled stiffly at each other for an awkward beat, both of us undoubtedly remembering the RIP JAINE AUSTEN headstone I'd found under Aidan's bed.

"About last night," Aidan finally said, breaking the silence. "I'm so sorry about that headstone. I was only trying to stop your investigation. But I swear, I didn't kill Misty."

The jury was still out on that one. For Lance's sake, I hoped Aidan wasn't the killer, but I wouldn't bet the rent on it.

"No worries," I fibbed. "We're good."

"So what can I get you? Bloody Mary? Zombie? Pepto Bismol?"

"Nothing, thanks. I'm fine."

I wasn't about to take any chances and have Aidan fix me something to drink. Not after unearthing that headstone.

"I guess I'll go mix and mingle with the hors d'oeuvres," I said, then tootled back to the buffet table to score some bagel bites.

By now, the volume on the sound track had been pumped up, and people had to raise their voices to be heard over the other-worldly moans and groans.

Noshing on a bagel bite, I saw Delia, regal as ever in a lush red cape, chatting with Preston and his wife. The two women were talking, animated. But Preston's eyes were wandering, sneaking glances at the two hottie influencers.

Why did I get the feeling his marriage was headed for divorce court?

Two bagel bites and a pizza pocket later, Delia said goodbye to Preston and his wife and walked over to a guest in a black cape, his hood pulled forward on his face.

Something about this guy looked familiar. I was certain I'd seen him somewhere before. Then it hit me. The man Delia had approached was the exterminator—the one who came to set mousetraps the day Misty was killed.

What the heck was he doing at the party?

Were David and Becca that desperate for guests?

"Corky!" I heard Delia exclaim. "I almost didn't recognize you with your hair covered up."

As the exterminator turned to greet Delia, the hood on his cape slipped off his head, revealing a mop of bright red hair. Omigosh, it was Corky MacLaine, the actor Preston had replaced, the guy who'd starred in the original *I Married a Zombie.*

He looked exactly like the exterminator. Only the exterminator had been bald.

And suddenly I wondered: What if the man I'd seen backstage that day wasn't really an exterminator? What if it had been Corky in disguise and the only pest he'd come to get rid of had been Misty?

Had he put on a bald cap, figuring nobody would recognize him without his famous head of thick red hair? But why would he want to kill Misty? He'd only worked with her for a few days.

Hold on. What if Corky *hadn't* donned a bald cap to disguise himself? Maybe Corky was actually bald, and his famous mop of hair was a wig. Maybe Misty discovered his secret and threatened to tell the world. She'd been more than eager to blackmail Preston. Who's to say she hadn't been blackmailing Corky, too?

Could it be? Was Corky the killer?

I looked up and saw him staring at me, a steely glint in his eyes. I didn't like that glint. Not one bit.

My cue to get the heck out of there.

Wasting no time, I dashed backstage to make my escape via the rusty side door. I was about to reach for the handle when I felt a hand clamp over mine.

I turned to see Corky and that scary glint in his eyes.

"You recognized me," he said, through gritted teeth.

"Of course, I recognize you!" I summoned up what I hoped was a convincing smile. "You're Corky MacLaine, beloved star of *I Married a Zombie*!"

"Cut the bull, Jaine. You saw me the day of Misty's murder, dressed as an exterminator. You didn't see through my disguise then, but I caught the way you were looking at me just now, and I'm afraid you've discovered the truth."

"Truth? What truth?" I asked, still playing dumb. "I have no idea what you're talking about."

But he wasn't buying it.

With an iron grip on my arm, he began dragging me to the prop area behind the stage.

"Help!" I cried at the top of my lungs.

"Don't waste your breath," Corky said. "No one can hear you over that sound track."

And he was right, of course. My screams were drowned out by those damn moans and groans.

I struggled to break free as he pulled me along, but Corky was stronger than me. A lot stronger. The guy was probably bench-pressing refrigerators. Try as I might, I couldn't escape his viselike grip. At one point, I managed to kick him, but he kicked me back with such force, I feared he might have fractured my shin bone.

All the while, he kept talking, still furious over what he claimed Misty had "forced" him to do.

"The scheming bitch caught me in my dressing room gluing on my wig and threatened to tell the world the truth about my hair. I paid ten grand to shut her up, but I knew that wouldn't be the end of it. And I wasn't about to pay her off for the rest of my life. So I took off my wig and showed up at the theater disguised as an exterminator to get rid of her for good. Misty knew too damn much, so she had to go.

"And so, I'm afraid, do you."

By now he'd dragged me past the prop headstones and over to the trapdoor Misty had used to lure Aidan down to the cellar for a make-out session.

"You're going down to the cellar. Only you won't be using the stairs. You're going to have a tragic accident and fall head first to your death."

Oh, lordy! I couldn't let this happen. Not without a fight. And not without tasting each and every one of Ben and Jerry's fifty-four flavors.

"This is it, Jaine," Corky was saying. "Time for your final exit."

Think again, Corky.

As he bent over to open the trapdoor, I reached down with my free hand and grabbed a fistful of Corky's bright red wig. I yanked it as hard as I could, wrenching it from his scalp, glue and all.

Now it was Corky's turn to scream.

Instinctively, he reached up to his bald dome in panic.

I took advantage of his momentary distress to whack him in the gut with a prop headstone, sending him sprawling on the floor.

Tossing his wig in his face, I began running for my life. I'd just made it past the prop area when I heard Corky clomping behind me. Dammit. Somehow he'd managed to get to his feet and was now hot on my heels.

I turned and saw his face, suffused with a murderous flush.

I had to stop him somehow.

Then I got an idea.

I whipped off my plastic zombie poncho and threw it in his path. Seconds later, I heard the gratifying sound of Corky cursing as he crashed to the floor. He'd tripped over the slick plastic, as I'd hoped he would.

With Corky down for the count, I raced onstage, hollering for help.

"What's wrong?" Becca cried, rushing up to me.

"Corky's the one who killed Misty. And just now, he tried to kill me. He was going to push me through the trapdoor down into the cellar."

"Oh, no!" Becca gasped.

"I'll go see if I can get him," Aidan said, racing backstage.

Seconds later, he returned with Corky wriggling in his grasp.

"I caught him at the side door, trying to put on this wig."

He waved Corky's red wig in the air.

"I always thought his hair was too good to be true," said Becca.

"I knew it was a rug the first time I saw him," Delia chimed in.

"Me too," said Preston.

"Me too," said Katie.

Omigosh, to think Corky had killed Misty for nothing. Everybody already knew the truth about his phony red mop.

By now, someone had called 911, and when the police came hustling into the theater, I filled them in on Corky's adventures as a part-time exterminator.

Corky, of course, denied everything, but then Preston piped up.

"Wait a minute," he said, staring at Corky. "I saw the exterminator when I went backstage to call my agent the day of the murder. It was Corky, all right."

That pretty much sealed the deal. Soon Corky was being hauled off to the B-list actors' wing of the county jail.

All around me, people were buzzing with excitement, the influencers posting like crazy. The story would be splashed all over the media, *I Married a Zombie* in the headlines.

The cops took down my statement in one of the dressing rooms, and when I returned to the stage, everyone rushed to congratulate me for having found the killer. One of the influencers even asked me if I could find her missing cat.

I got hugs from Becca and all the cast members, Aidan whispering in my ear, "I told you it wasn't me!"

Even David managed a weak smile.

"Let me get you a drink," Katie offered.

"No, thanks. I'm beat."

And I was. Near-death experiences tend to tucker me out.

I said my goodbyes and headed for the exit. In spite of the pain in my shin from Corky's vicious kick, I was feeling quite chipper.

True, my days as a script doctor were a bit of a disaster, and my chances of getting that prestigious gig with the Pasadena society gals were practically nil.

But who cared?

I was alive, I was ambulatory, and I was walking out of the theater with a pocket full of bagel bites.

You've Got Mail

To: Jausten
From: Shoptillyoudrop
Subject: Sweet as Pie

I thought I'd never forgive Daddy after the talent show fiasco. But I can't ever seem to stay mad at him for long. He's been sweet as pie, bought me roses and a big box of peanut butter fudge. Not to mention a divine dinner at Le Chateaubriand, Tampa Vistas's most elegant restaurant, where I had steak and molten chocolate lava cake for dessert.

Best news of all, animal protection services took custody of Iggy and released him to his natural habitat, where I'm sure he's much happier sitting in the sun than he ever was on Daddy's head.

XOXO,
Mom

To: Jausten
From: DaddyO
Subject: Farewell to Iggy

Sad news, Lambchop. I've had to say goodbye to my buddy Iggy. It was with a heavy heart that I watched him being carted off by the animal control people.

But, as Mom says, I'm sure he'll be happier in his new home, far from the clutches of the Battle Axe. (I'm still convinced she was the one who let him loose.)

Meanwhile, I've got his tiny top hat on the fireplace mantel. A treasured memento of our time together.

Love 'n kisses,
Daddy

To: Jausten
From: Shoptillyoudrop
Subject: Heaven!

It's been sheer heaven not having to listen to Daddy tappity-tap-tapping. Peace and quiet at last!

XOXO,
Mom

To: Jausten
From: DaddyO

Guess what, Lambchop? I figured out what I'm going to do for next year's talent show, an act that's sure to wow everyone.

I'm going to learn to play the trumpet!

I bought one used on eBay from a guy who swears it used to belong to Louis Armstrong. It's coming tomorrow. Don't tell Mom. I want to surprise her.

Love 'n munches from
Daddy

Epilogue

Alas, in spite of all the publicity swirling around the show, *I Married a Zombie* closed six nights after it opened (which was five more nights than I'd given it). By the final performance, there were more people onstage than in the audience.

But that didn't stop Becca and Katie. Bitten by the theater bug, they put together a one-woman show for Katie called *Cryptessa and Me*, which turned out to be a smash hit.

Next week, it's opening off-Broadway.

Becca and Katie have moved to New York for the run of the show. And they're not the only ones newly relocated to the Big Apple.

One of the few people who turned up to see *I Married a Zombie* was an agent who was so impressed by Aidan's performance as Uncle Dedly, he signed him as a client and got him a gig on a New York soap opera. So now Aidan is living in Greenwich Village, not far from Becca and Katie, and dating the soap's set designer.

In the Poetic Justice department, Becca dumped David when she caught him sexting with a wannabe actress, who in turn dumped him when his lottery winnings ran out.

Last I heard, he was working at Pizza Hut.

I was right about Preston's marriage. He and his child

bride split up soon after the "Come as a Zombie" party. Much to my surprise, he's been dating an age-appropriate woman. And you'll never guess who it is: Delia! That's right. The two thespians fell for each other on the set of *I Married a Zombie* and are currently touring the country in *Love Letters*.

Lance was in mourning for several torturous weeks after Aidan moved to New York, milking his heartbreak for all it was worth, but quickly flew out of his depression when he met his "love for all eternity" at the gym. Eternity, in that case, turned out to be twenty-seven days.

As for Kandi, she finally got to take her maiden voyage on Ethan's yacht, where she promptly got seasick, up-chucking into one of Ethan's treasured yachting trophy cups. Not surprisingly, the relationship fizzled out once they touched land.

Here at Casa Austen, I've given up walking Prozac. It was costing me a fortune in Kitty Kaviar treats. And besides, she's eaten so darn many of them, she doesn't fit in her harness anymore. I'm happy to report she hasn't once snuck out of the apartment to raid Mrs. Hurlbutt's kitchen. (Although she did manage to poop on her prize petunias.)

And I'm back writing for Toiletmasters, more than happy to be reunited with my good buddy, the double-flush commode.

Needless to say, I never got that job with the Pasadena Historical Society. They did, however, offer me discount tickets to one of their house tours.

Speaking of the Pasadena Historical Society, guess who just called? Ward, the old coot from the board of directors. He wants to take me to dinner at a crazy-expensive seafood restaurant in Santa Monica called The Lobster.

Well, if you think I'm going to go out with someone old enough to be my grandfather just for a free lobster dinner, you're absolutely right! He's picking me up at eight.

I'll let you know how it goes.

XOXO

PS. Skyler sold his pfork on *Shark Tank* for $1.4 million and is now living in a Bel Air mansion with a gal he met at a funeral reception.